In the
Wake
of
Betrayal

ANNA RAINS

Prime Seven Media
518 Landmann St.
Tomah City, WI 54660

Printed in the United States of America

Table of Contents

Chapter 1

The man knew where he was going. He had instructions to kidnap a little boy. The day was carefully chosen when the child was unlikely to be overly supervised. It was the day of the Great Annual Open Garden Fete and Funfair held in the grounds of an old manor house in Wiltshire, and his mother was in charge of the whole thing.

The house and gardens originally belonged to her parents, both now dead, but Helen had insisted on keeping up the tradition because it was the highlight for the whole village and indeed surrounding villages and towns. People drove for miles to take part in the festivities on offer. The annual event took place every year on the Sunday of the May Bank holiday, this year the last Sunday in May.

Helen got up soon after 5am. As she drew back the curtains, she realised it was going to be a glorious day. The sun was rising rapidly above the horizon and the slight mist hovering over the grass foretold of a warm, if not hot, day. She smiled knowing the fete would be crowded and the charity, her local hospice, was going to receive a bumper donation.

She didn't bother putting on a robe and headed straight for the bathroom. Opening the window wide, Helen breathed in the fresh morning air and stood for a few minutes listening to the sound of the birds, singing and twittering while going about their business of nest building.

It was going to be perfect. No hitches this year – she hoped, smiling as she remembered the previous year when they had run out of milk in the tea tent, and someone had been sent scurrying to the shop to buy more. No problem with that this year, she'd made sure they had more than ample supplies. She prayed nothing would go wrong.

Showered, she pulled her hair back into a ponytail, put on shorts, a bright shirt and sandals, before heading downstairs. The house was full of guests. Her sister Alison and brother-in-law Rory had come to help, as they always did. Her PA was also in residence and numerous other friends and relatives.

As Helen was pouring herself a coffee to take out to check on everything, she was surprised to see Alison join her in the kitchen.

"Hi Sis, what are you doing up so early?"

"Same as you, I guess. Couldn't sleep and thought I would have a wander around. Is there any more coffee in the pot?"

"The machine is turned on. Help yourself", answered Helen.

The two sisters made their way out through the back door to begin their inspection. Apart from the sound of the birdsong, the two sisters walked in silence.

Later, Helen spoke, "I am not expecting anything to go wrong today. As you know everything has been meticulously planned. Daddy would have been so pleased".

"You've done an amazing job Helen, and besides what is going to go wrong?"

Neither of the sisters could possibly envisage the nightmare that would occur before too many hours passed.

By 7.30am people began to arrive. The fair ground workers emerged from their caravans and began checking everything. Tea ladies opened the marquee, while carpark attendants chatted about how to control the influx of cars and vans that would be arriving. The Bacon Butty van opened for business and began selling bacon rolls, the scent of which drew in more early morning shoppers. Everyone was excited and looking forward to a busy day.

Everything was in place. Back at the manor house, guests were having breakfast. Rory was overseeing the entry fee at the gate to the carpark, later telling Helen at the staggering increase in visitors.

The first hitch was a problem in the tea tent. Someone had switched off the power line, causing a panic among the ladies manning it. The urns for hot water were not heating up. Nobody admitted to being anywhere near the power socket. Later, much later the police wondered if this had been done deliberately to cause a distraction.

Then one of the rides got stuck with people left sitting in their seats. The fairground workers were 'puzzled' not finding the problem immediately. Was it an accident, or had somebody tampered with it?

Nobody noticed a grey-haired elderly man wearing a baseball cap loitering near the tea tent where he followed an electric cable between the tent and the nearby shed. Slipping inside he quietly unplugged the plug from the socket. Smiling to himself he left, prepared to say he'd been looking for the gents if anyone had asked him why he had entered the building. He then headed for his next place to sabotage – one of the rides where he sauntered round the back and simply pulled the lever to the off position. He knew both should cause confusion and hoped that the boy's mother would be too busy to keep an eye on her son – his target.

Helen was everywhere trying to help sort out what was happening – her day was beginning to go badly.

Chapter 2

ernard arrived in good time. He'd insisted on parking near the exit, which was at the other end of the field so he could get away without going near the entrance, muttering he had to leave early and didn't want to get blocked in. He'd dressed carefully. Nothing to make him stand out so that people might remember him.

Jeans, trainers and a plain grey t-shirt with no distinctive designs, a baseball cap and sunglasses completed his outfit.

He knew exactly who he was looking for. He'd been given a photo of the child. While he didn't totally agree with the plot, he'd been offered enough money to make it worthwhile.

He wandered through the crowds looking for his prey, while causing distractions as the police eventually guessed. Anything to cause the boy's mother to take her eyes off her son. Then he spotted him, an eight-year-old boy with a bright red t-shirt, heading towards the burger van. Bernard followed him and managed, with a bit of queue jumping, to get behind Hugo. The line was quite long with so many people choosing to buy lunch at the same time, for themselves and in many cases, a whole family, all wanting different things.

Bernard found it easy to get into a conversation with the young boy, who was already over excited.

"Your parents sent you over to get a burger?"

"No, my mum is organising everything and she is busy, so she gave me some money to buy myself something".

"Your mum must be very clever. It is a huge event".

"Yes, she is", replied Hugo proudly. "This used to be my granddad's house, but he died about three years ago and since then we have big family holidays here".

"What's your name son?"

"Hugo. Hugo Brierly and I've got a sister too".

By the time they had reached to front of the queue. Bernard, although he hadn't told Hugo his name, suggested they sat down on a bench to eat what they had each ordered.

"What about that seat over there?" suggested Bernard, pointing to one a bit out of the way. They sat down together with their backs to what was going on. Bernard did not want anyone to get a close look at him.

Over the next half an hour Bernard drew much more out of the boy. He learnt that his parents were divorced, and he didn't know where his dad was. He understood his dad had done something bad and wasn't allowed to see him anymore. He knew his mother was cross with dad, but he didn't know why. He also found out that Hugo was very proud of his grandfather.

"Granddad was a writer. He wrote the book, 'The Unending War' about a spy, and they made it into a film. Mum got to go to the Oscars with my grandparents. The film got lots of Oscars and made my granddad a millionaire – at least that's what I overheard one day. He wrote lots of other books as well and so he was famous!"

"You are very lucky. I grew up in a very poor family. We didn't have anything. Do you miss your dad?"

"Yes, we did lots of fun things together. I'm sorry I can't see him now. Dad told me he would take me to a Spurs match, Tottenham Hotspurs", he explained in case the old man didn't understand. "They are dad's favourite team".

"Would you like to see your father?"

"I would, but I am not allowed. Mum won't let Amy or me near him. She says she doesn't trust him. Mum and me and Amy are going to California in the summer – as soon as we get out of school. Mum has a friend over there – someone she met when she was helping granddad with his books. Mandy, the mum, has three children about the same ages as me and Amy. She lives in a big house near LA. They've got a huge swimming pool – just for them, and mum says we can swim in it all day if we want".

"That sounds great!"

Hugo added, "We've got a swimming pool here, but it's not very big. And we are going to Disneyland and Sea World in San Diego, and mum says we are *not* sitting in the front row because when the whale jumps out of the water, it causes a tidal wave and everybody at the front gets wet!" Hugo chatted on to his new friend. "And they've got really big rides at Disneyland, not like these small ones here! I can't wait. Mum says she will go on the big ones with me, but Amy can't 'cos she's too little".

Bernard interrupted, "I know your dad. At least, I have met him. He has always said he loved you very much indeed. He is very ill. Not long to live, and he has said he would love to see you again – before he dies".

Hugo glanced up at him. Was he telling the truth? At this moment Bernard produced his trump card – a photo of Hugo's father.

"He told me that if I was ever fortunate enough to meet you, please would I give you his picture".

"That's dad! Where is he?"

"Not very far from here right now. I could take you there. It wouldn't take very long".

"What about mum? I'd have to ask her if it is OK and maybe, if she knows that he is dying, she wouldn't mind".

"What do you think? From what I've heard about your mum from your dad James, I don't think she would agree. Look, this thing will be going on for hours and we could be gone and back again in a very short time, so she doesn't have to know". Hugo hesitated. He knew his mother would say no – but he had loved his dad very much indeed, and if his dad was very ill, he might never see him again. So, he agreed to go with Bernard, who seemed a really nice old man. He didn't see the silent punch in the air that Bernard did. Bernard smiled to himself thinking how funny James would find it to hear he was 'dying'.

That was when Bernard produced his second trick. He pulled out a Tottenham Hotspur team shirt in Hugo's size. It even had the number of his dad's favourite player on the back, number 7.

"Your dad always wanted to take you to see a game played by his favourite team?" Hugo nodded; his eyes glued to the shirt. "Your dad gave this to me and asked me to give it to you. In fact, he would like to see you wearing it, so take off your red t-shirt and put this Spurs shirt on – especially for him".

Hugo quickly reached out for the shirt while pulling off his top. Bernard took the t-shirt while Hugo was hastily putting on the new one – his eyes shining. Bernard shoved the old shirt under his arm while discreetly pinning a note on to it. This was going to be left behind for them to find. Not too quickly, he wanted to get away before the search began.

The note read: *We've got your son, Hugo. If you value his life, you must find £3 million by Friday 4.30pm. We will tell you how to get it to us in the next few days. Take this seriously. Do not tell anyone – especially the police.*

"Come on Hugo, let's go and surprise your dad".

As they walked away, Bernard bent down as if to tie his shoelace, while pushing the shirt under a bush, not so far in it wouldn't be visible by people looking for the child, and everybody would be looking for a child in a red t-shirt and not one dressed in a white and blue football shirt.

The person behind the planning, knew exactly what they were doing!

Chapter 3

It had been a very long day, with record takings. Her PA, who oversaw the money, was going to leave it until the next day to tot up the takings. Rory, Alison's husband, had volunteered to help.

Then Helen became aware that she hadn't seen Hugo for hours. This wasn't like him, usually he popped up all over the place asking for money for something to eat or to go on one of the rides.

She began to ask around, but nobody had seen him since lunch time. Helen began to panic. She ran round the garden asking everyone if they had seen him and nobody had. By this time, she was in a terrible state. Rory found her dashing from one place to another.

"Helen let's organise this properly. I'll get everyone still here to look for him. He must be here somewhere".

But Helen had a deep down, gut feeling that something seriously wrong had happened to her son.

Alison took her into the house and told her she would be better waiting for news rather than dashing around all over the place. It was soon after this that Rory came in holding a red shirt. Helen went white.

"That's Hugo's. Where did you find it?"

"Partly tucked under a bush. There's a note pinned to it. I haven't opened it – would you like me to?

"Yes. No, give it to me". With hands that were shaking so much she could scarcely undo the pin, Rory stood behind her, looking over her shoulder, while Helen opened the small piece of paper. She reacted the way the kidnapper expected in shock, fear etched all over her face.

"Oh my God Rory. What can I do? Where can they have taken Hugo?"

Rory pushed her down into a chair. "The first thing we have to do it to call the police".

"We can't! They are threatening to kill Hugo if we do!"

"We have to Helen. The police have special units to deal with kidnappings. They are trained to work undercover and will make no moves to show they are involved. I will make some discreet calls. I am sure we'll find him safe and sound very soon."

Helen began screaming, "Where's Amy? Where is she?", as she jumped up.

Alison had returned, "It's OK Helen, she's fine. She's with the other children and I have asked a couple of the other guests to stay with them".

Helen was sobbing uncontrollably now, while Rory was trying to find the right person in the police force to help them. This wasn't easy as he didn't want to give too much away, afraid the kidnappers were still around and might take action against Hugo. Eventually he told Helen that an Inspector Colin Jarvis was on his way and bringing a female policewoman with him. He couldn't say how long it would be as he was based in London but would get here as quickly as possible.

"Is there anything we can do while we are waiting?" asked Rory.

Inspector Jarvis replied, "Yes, between you write down everything you can think of – the more in depth as possible. Get everyone in the house and those you can trust who were with you today, to make notes – especially when they last saw the child. Anything will do".

Rory told him about the shirt and the note, and the inspector told him not to allow anyone else to touch it.

They could only wait and pray.

Chapter 4

ernard and Hugo walked for a few minutes until they came to Bernard's van, parked very near the exit to the field. Nobody else was anywhere near because all the action was taking place at the entrance, where cars were still lining up to enter. This is exactly what Bernard had hoped.

"Hop in Hugo, it won't be long before we see your dad. He's staying at your uncle's house, not far away. Do your seat belt up".

"I didn't know I had another uncle – only Uncle Rory."

"Well, you do. You see your mummy has got two brothers, half-brothers, which she never knew anything about. They are both older than her."

"But if they are older than her, why didn't she know about them?"

"Your granny, Mummy's mum, was your grandfather's second wife. He had been married before but when he divorced his first wife, he never saw her or his two sons again. Look, we are getting close, so I will tell you all about it on the way back".

Bernard avoided saying any more and half an hour later, turned into a side street and pulling up in front of a small terrace house.

"Here we are son, let's go in and meet some other members of your family."

Hugo was curious but still puzzled. Why didn't mum know about her brothers? Why hadn't they come round and visited them like Aunt Alison and Uncle Rory, he wondered.

Bernard got out of his van and went round to help Hugo out. "Come on Hugo, let's go."

Bernard knocked on the front door, which opened almost immediately, as if someone was expecting them to arrive.

"Hello Bernard" an older man said, "Come on in. Who's that with you?"

"Hello Keith, this is Hugo, James's son. Say hello to your Uncle Keith, Hugo."

Hugo just muttered "Hello." He just didn't know what was going on. "Where's my dad, this man told me I was coming to see my dad?" He was now becoming quite agitated. "I want to see my dad!"

"It's alright Hugo, your dad will be here soon".

At this the man, called Keith, stared forcefully at Bernard, while thinking, 'what the hell is he on about'. James wasn't coming and as far as he knew he was in France.

Bernard led Hugo inside the house. A lady came to meet him. She was a bit younger than his mum. She had a nice face, and she was smiling at him. Hugo smiled back. He noticed that she was taller than his mother and had much darker hair.

"Hugo, this is your cousin Janet, perhaps you'd better call her Auntie Janet though."

"Hello," said Auntie Janet. "It's really nice to meet you, Hugo. I never met my grandfather, but I know you have the same name as he did."

Hugo frowned. How could she have the same grandfather as he did? She was much older than he was. It didn't make sense.

Auntie Janet continued, "Would you like to come and meet some other cousins?" and she took him through the house into the back garden where three children were playing. A boy, who looked as though he was about the same age as Hugo, and two younger sisters.

"Hugo, this is Sophie, she's five; Michael, who is nine and Eliza is seven." Turning to the children she said, "Come and meet your cousin and make him feel at home. His uncle says he will be staying with us for a few days."

Hugo felt panicky. "But I'd rather stay with my mummy," he blurted out.

"Of course, but your uncle says that your dad has asked him to bring you here for a little while. Don't worry Hugo we are not going to hurt you, and you'll be back with her very soon. Your dad told us he's got a surprise for your mum."

His Uncle Keith came out into the garden at that moment and said quietly to his daughter Janet, "Bernard says James is on his way, which I don't believe. Much more likely Bernard is going to have to drive all the way to the cottage in France, where James, will pretend he doesn't know what's going on, and blames it all on Bernard".

"I want my mum! Please take me back to my mummy!" wailed Hugo.

"We will shortly", said Keith, gently, "we will get you home very soon, don't you worry. "You just go and play with Michael in his bedroom for a while."

Hugo went off with Michael, still sniffing, but still believing that mummy was going to get a nice surprise.

"Now," said Janet, "what is going on? First, you drag us down here - for a few days you said. Then Bernard suddenly turns up with a cousin I scarcely know anything about! What the hell is going on?" She was almost shouting at her father. "And, where the hell did my Uncle Bernard go off to? He said he was going to Scotland. How come he's back here and bringing James's son with him?"

Keith pulled her over to him. "Please don't shout. It's not my idea; it's James and Bernard's plan. I don't like it, but I seem to be involved. All we must do is to look after Hugo for a few days. James says if we do, we'll get a million pounds."

"A million pounds!" screamed Janet. "If James is involved it's got to be crooked! I don't want anything to do with it. Why is he behaving this way? Why does he hate Helen so much? I thought he'd already got a million pounds and a cottage in France out of her."

"I don't *know* why!" exclaimed Keith. "All I know is that James wanted us to help, and he said we would be set up for life. Please Janet, just help me for a few days. Look after Hugo and for God's sake *don't* say a word to anybody!"

"You've got to tell me more. Bernard takes James's son away from the child's mother, then he comes and dumps him on us, and now I want you to tell me what the bloody hell your brother, James is up to. I've never ever trusted James, he's too smarmy by half! Why dad? Why are we involved with him and what's obviously a very nasty scheme?"

"James in not my brother, nor Bernard's either, he's a half-brother. Same mother but different father. And I can't tell you anymore. I've said - I just don't know what they are up to. Believe me, Jan, I think we must go along with them at the moment because I think *we'd* be in big trouble if we didn't"

"For crying out loud dad, I've had it up to here with this rotten family, not you of course, but Bernard and James. I just think you are so weak to have been drawn in. But the other two are greedy, vengeful and rotten! I wish we weren't mixed up in this mess." With that she burst into tears. Her father put his arms around her. She pushed him away and said angrily, "Just get us the fuck out of it! Otherwise, I will call the police."

At that moment the back door opened and in walked 'uncle' Bernard'. Janet put her hand over her mouth and ran into the kitchen.

"Everything went well. We were lucky though – I didn't have to disturb Helen. She was so busy being in charge, and with one or two 'distractions' I created, she was much too involved to notice Hugo's disappearance. I found a neat way to deliver the ransom note. So here we go – on our way to get rich".

"I don't want any of the filthy money! You are a bastard Bernard, and a fool to have anything to do with James. I know you are not the brightest, but if you think you are going to get away with this, you are wrong. Why do you think James was having nothing to do with the actual kidnap? Because he was setting you up. Don't you understand, James never, ever does anything for anybody else? He's been bad from the day he was born. He's a psychopath, he enjoys hurting people, always has done. He doesn't care who he hurts, not you, not me and my family, he only thinks of himself and what he wants. Let me tell you, Bernard, it'll be you going to prison – not James. That smarmy bastard will have planned it all along, that you get caught – not him! Oh my God, Bernard why the hell did you have to get involved? And much worse, why did you drag Janet and me and my grandchildren into it?

Bernard didn't answer immediately because he was struck by what his brother Keith had said. So, he wasn't the brightest? He would show them.

"I'll be gone in the morning, taking Hugo with me". What he didn't say was that Keith's words had hit home, and Bernard was already changing his plans. He'd make his half-brother James see what he could do. He'd show him. Show them all!

"Where are you going?"

"I think I'll keep that to myself at the moment – just in case you have any ideas of telling anyone else".

"Who do you think I'd tell?"

"I don't know, but you might".

Later Keith sat on the side of his bed with tears running down his cheeks saying to himself, "Oh God I am so sorry for that poor woman, not because she is my half-sister whom I have never met, but the pain she must be going through because of the sheer cruelty of my two brothers".

He thought of calling the police, and for the rest of his life, he didn't know why he hadn't done so. He believed it was because of his fear of being implicated in the kidnap. He didn't know what plans Bernard had, and he didn't want to know. Just let the little boy be safe, that's all, let Hugo be safe. He never even thought about calling James and demanding an answer.

Chapter 5

Alison and Rory struggled to keep Helen from marching up and down the room, with tears running down her cheeks, berating herself for being such a bad mother. How could she have just let Hugo out of her sight, and crying out wondering where the child was and giving way to her fears for his safety?

"Who could be cruel enough?"

Both Rory and Alison kept quiet about their thoughts. There was only one person, in their opinion and that was her former husband James, and it would be time enough to express them when the Inspector arrived, which he did sooner than they had expected. It turned out he'd come in an unmarked police car, driven at speed, with blue lights flashing until it got close to the manor house. With him was the female policewoman who he introduced as Sergeant Jill Wood.

Noticing Helen's concern about the police getting involved, he gently told her that his department were trained in this sort of thing and knew that secrecy was vital.

Turning to Rory he said, "I have a number of plain clothed colleagues following on. They are needed to take statements and to conduct a search of the grounds. Did you ask everyone here to start making notes about what they had seen?"

Rory nodded and indicated some papers lying on the big desk. "It hasn't been easy to get very far as my sister-in-law is extremely upset at the moment".

"The sergeant will take over now sir. Is there another room where you and your wife could go to continue your reports?"

"Yes, next door. I have arranged for coffee and some sandwiches to be brought in here for you. Mrs Stevens, our cook is still up and insists on doing what she can to help".

"Thank you. Right, sergeant, would you like to bring Mrs Brierly over to the sofa and we can begin."

Helen agreed, as she felt she could trust these two. The sergeant put a mug of hot coffee in her hands, although to begin with she was shaking so much she was afraid she would spill the liquid all over herself. The warmth of the coffee seemed to help her calm down a little.

"Now Mrs Brierly, could you in your own time, go through exactly what happened today".

Rory had come back into the room to join them, Alison was still writing her notes and helping others with theirs, he said.

Helen went through the day, telling them what she remembered,

"I got up, around 5.30 I think and showered and dressed for the day, then Ali and I took our coffee to wader round the garden to make sure everything was in place for the day ahead. Everything was well organised, and we both thought that nothing could go wrong", at this point she was unable to say any more except calling out Hugo's name in an anguished voice. The sergeant took notes while the interview was recorded.

"Do you have any idea who might have done it, Mrs Brierly?"

"I hate the name Brierly!"

The inspector's eyebrows lifted slightly, wondering why she was so adamant. I'll find out later, he thought.

"I don't know, but the only person I know nasty enough is my ex-husband, James. He has been after me for more money – I think he has large gambling debts. He's tried numerous ways to persuade me to give him more money".

"'Tell me about him".

Helen wondered where to begin. She swallowed hard before starting to speak.

"I suppose it will be easier to go from the beginning. I met James at a party in London. I was up staying with a girl I had been to college with. We did theatre studies together at Bristol. It was a couple of hours drive from home – you see my father finally settled down in Wiltshire, near Salisbury. Anyway, I went up to London for the weekend to stay with Sally - Sally Newley. We had both gone our separate ways when we left college. She went off to Edinburgh where she got to know some people who were involved in the Festival and sort of joined them. I was never quite sure what she did, but she had a great deal of fun – especially with things connected with the Edinburgh Fringe."

"After a couple of years Sally met a charming Scotsman called Angus McLeod who owned and ran a hotel on the edge of some loch. Before long she seemed to be surrounded by children and dogs. Well, actually only three children, but numerous dogs! She and Angus make a great couple. Sally has been wonderful in the hotel. We love going there and are planning to go for New Year again this year…. Oh gosh what will we do if we haven't found Hugo by then?"

Another huge sigh escaped from Helen. "Where was I? I'm not boring you, am I?"

"No, this all very helpful to get an insight of your background. You were saying how you had met James," said the inspector softly.

"Oh yes. I went up to London to stay for a long weekend – this was to be a sort of a 'Hen Party' weekend because Sally was getting married about four weeks later."

"May I ask what work you were doing at the time Mrs Brierly?"

"I was working for my father. I never did anything with my theatre studies, unlike Sally. I finished college, went off to Hong Kong to stay with my godmother for three months and then came home and joined my father."

"What did your father do?"

"Oh, he was a writer – he wrote many mystery books – a kind of a Len Deighton. My father's name was Douglas Smith. I did all the typing and editing for him. He never got going with word processors or computers. He preferred to either write things down in longhand or dictate them straight to me. You see it was something I could continue to do even after I had the children."

"And your husband Mrs Brierly, perhaps we can get back to him", gently prodded the inspector.

"Please could you call me Helen, I feel more comfortable with my Christian name, especially now if we are considering that my former husband may be involved?"

"Certainly Mrs Br…. Helen. Would it help if you called me Colin, my Christian name?"

Helen nodded and continued talking. She had forgotten about Sergeant Jill Wood who was sitting quietly in the corner taking notes.

"Sally had invited quite a lot of old friends to her parent's flat. It wasn't going to be 'a girls' weekend, sort of thing, no strippers or anything like that. More like friends who had known her since she was a baby, godparents and the like. One of her friends turned out to be James. Sally laughingly told me to keep clear of him, that he was charming, but a bit of a rogue! I wish now that I had listened to her!"

"James was so attractive" she went on, "same colouring as Hugo. His hair had been blonde when he was a little boy, he said, but when I first met him it had turned to a sort of deep honey tone. His eyes are a greenish/hazel colour. He made everyone laugh. Actually, it was much later when I realised that although James laughed a lot, it was only his mouth that expressed warmth, while his eyes remained cold.

He still has a very quick wit. I think I fell in love with him that night. He seemed so right for me. Tall, handsome and interested in so many things I enjoyed doing. He was a graphic designer – had finished college and done two years in Paris, which is why his French is so fluent. We talked about all manner of things – our love of the theatre and design; about my father's writing and my mother's impracticality. My mother was very, very intelligent but not practical at all. My friends used to laugh about some of the meals she dished up – but they came to visit her anyway! She loved 'discussing things'– but we always said she enjoyed a 'good argument'. Pity she never went into politics – she would have been brilliant. Actually, James is beginning to lose some of his hair now and I think he feels that he's getting old!"

"Anyway, James made a beeline for me. I wondered later if he knew how wealthy my father was and was using me. You see, James didn't really have much affection for anyone but himself. Except Hugo because Hugo is an extension of himself."

"James and I left the party together and walked along the embankment. He made me laugh so much. We walked until dawn and then he returned me to Sally's flat."

"We all met at lunchtime on the Sunday, the day after the party. I don't remember where, but it was a pub overlooking the river. Again we talked almost exclusively. He asked a lot of questions about my father, our home, our lifestyle." Helen kept pausing while she thought about her early life.

"The following weekend, I took him down to meet my parents and my sister. To be fair, my mother thoroughly enjoyed meeting him, but I felt that my father was a bit reserved. At the time I thought my father was a little jealous of him because I had always been my father's favourite, being his first child. He was quite a bit older than Mummy; twelve years, he was forty-nine when I was born. But later, after I got to know James well, I realised that my father was always a good judge of character and had seen through James even then.

"James and I were hardly apart after that. He was so attentive to me – and to Mummy! Always bringing her flowers and presents. James always liked to be the centre of attraction.

"There was one occasion when a former boyfriend turned up at home. He had really come to see my parents, but James became extremely jealous and when we were alone later, he twisted my arm quite sharply and said "You belong to me and don't you forget it!" I cried myself to sleep that night. He was so apologetic next day and said he'd had too much to drink so I forgave him."

"I remember that evening" interrupted Rory, "I thought he had one heck of a cheek considering he had been chatting up other women all night! - your father was disturbed by his behaviour."

"I know, Daddy tried to tell me what James was like – he said he wanted me to be as happy with my future partner as he was with Mummy. I just replied that James was wonderful and that I *was* just as happy as he and Mummy were. Daddy looked a little sad – and I thought he was getting old because he had turned seventy-four."

"Anyway, we got married the following year when I was twenty-five and James was twenty-eight. My parents gave us a wonderful wedding and James showed me Paris on our honeymoon. On our return I went back to work for my father. At this time he was very busy writing. One of his books had been turned into a very successful movie. It was called 'The Unending War' about a spy in the Cold War between the U.S. and Russia.

"I remember that one," said the inspector; "didn't it win about seven Oscars?"

"Yes, and as my father had a share of the profits, the money was literally pouring in. It was at this time that James began to ask me to persuade my father to set him up in business. To begin with my father refused, but when he saw how upset I got, he told James to get a business plan together and he would look at it."

The inspector's phone went off at this moment. "Will you excuse me while I answer this?"

Helen nodded and said that perhaps she would like another cup of coffee now. Rory got up to make cups for all four of them.

In the corner of the room Inspector Jarvis answered his mobile.

"Has Hugo been found?" She cried out.

What he didn't tell Helen was that Rory had provided him with James's telephone number, and he had arranged for a French speaking colleague to phone the cottage in France but so far the policewoman had had no response. She was going to pretend she dialled the wrong number. Could Mr James Brierly have been involved in the kidnapping his own son? Rory had offered to go over to France early next morning and the inspector hoped they would find the child there.

However, now there wasn't anything they could do until the kidnapper came forward again with a ransom demand and then they could begin to close the net. He didn't really believe that the child was in danger. Paedophiles don't normally send cryptic notes to the parents – they just made off with the child for their own evil behaviours!

"Perhaps you could give us a full description of your husband Helen? His height, colouring, type of car he drives – photographs, if you have any with you? Anything that might help."

"I don't think there is anything in the house here. My father wouldn't have anything that reminded him of what a nasty piece of work I married. I only have a small one. It's really only a snapshot of him with Hugo when we all went skiing a couple of years ago. Actually only James and Hugo went skiing - I am not very keen and anyway I had to look after Amy."

While she was talking, she was opening up her handbag and wallet to pull out a small photograph. "I'm sorry it's not very good because

James is wearing a ski hat and sunglasses and Hugo's got goggles on. I can get something later. I am sure daddy will have had some photos of us all somewhere."

"I know we have better photographs than that", said Rory. "Look, how would it be if I drive home to find some decent photos – I could drop them off here on my way to the channel tunnel on my way to France?"

He turned to Helen, "Yes, I have spoken to the inspector, and we have agreed for me to go to the cottage in Maligny. James may be surprised to see me, but I have used the cottage as a stopping off place on my way back from buying wine, especially Chablis. So, hopefully he won't be suspicious".

"That's a good idea, sir. I will still be here and I can circulate any information you've got".

Rory went out of the room to talk to Alison and to reassure her that Helen had the sergeant, Jill, who would be with her, or within speaking distance.

"She seems to be a very sensible woman and will get more from Helen than we can. I'll say goodnight to Helen for you. You go off to bed now, Helen is going to need you".

"Helen", said Inspector Jarvis gently, "you must try and get some rest. Rory will be on his way shortly and I have to go back to my office – there are things I have to put in place. He'll be back here in a couple of hours or so, having collected anything that might be useful, before heading to France. Sergeant Jill Wood will remain here with you."

Helen shook her head. "I'd rather be on my own. I don't want anyone here watching every move I make."

"Don't worry, Jill will be very discreet, but we cannot leave you here on your own, and in case the kidnapper happens to make contact again, I want the sergeant to act as a witness. I have to stress that we don't know who the kidnapper is, we are guessing that it is your ex-husband,

and I certainly hope it is. I don't believe he would harm you son – it's the money he wants!"

Rory chipped in, "I'm off now. Will be back in a couple of hours or so, on my way to the tunnel. I'll go now and if James has got Hugo, for whatever reason, I'll phone you immediately. I hope to be in Chablis soon after lunch. I'll be catching an early ferry."

"This is my mobile phone number, Helen," said the inspector, "if anything happens either you or Jill can phone me day or night – I don't care what time it is. Good night and try and get some rest. I will also be back in a few hours".

Chapter 6

elen closed the door behind him. She felt completely devastated. Was it only six hours since the nightmare had begun? It must be because it was just 10.00p.m. She sat down on the sofa still dressed in the clothes she had worn for the garden event. She couldn't bear the thought of preparing for bed with Hugo out there somewhere.

Sergeant Jill Wood, quietly made her a cup of tea and went through to the room next door, where she also remained dressed. She wanted to be in hearing distance of Helen, but to give her some space at the same time.

Helen thought of all the times when she had read about, or seen on television, reports of other children who had gone missing. She had believed she could put herself in their mother's place. She thought she could feel their fears and terror, but she knew now she was wrong. It was far, far worse when it was your own child. The pain was crippling. She kept thinking how terrified Hugo must be. Had he been crying for her? Had they given him food and water? How had they got him away? Oh God, not in the boot of a car! Where was he now? Was he in a dark cellar or some other frightening place? Details of some of her father's books came back to her in terrifying reality. No good saying to herself that her father had made up the stories. The stories seemed real – even more so now when it was happening to her. There was one where a child had been kidnapped and hidden in a storage room in an underground car park. Thousands of people had driven past for days before they found the child. It turned out that the father worked there and had taken the child during a marriage dispute. But it wasn't like that with her and James – *if* James was involved, or was it? She'd never been difficult about his having access to the children. Oh yes, after her father died and left his fortune to her and her sister – some £27 million and constantly growing from film rights and royalties, she did have a problem with James. He had threatened to take the children away permanently, unless she gave him a considerable share of the money.

No, it couldn't be that. She had given him the house in France and agreed to a £1 million settlement if he would accept an amicable divorce. It was far more than her father would have wanted, but Helen felt that as James was the father of her children and, as she didn't want any more trouble, she decided to be generous.

She hadn't told the inspector, Colin Jarvis, about James saying he would take the children – but could it be this deep down, gut feeling that he was quite capable of doing something like this, had stopped her from phoning him again. At least Rory would be in France tomorrow to prove one way or another whether James was involved.

She didn't remember falling asleep or maybe just dozing off when she was jerked awake by the sound of the telephone ringing on the desk in front of her. The light was still on and so she had no difficulty in finding the phone. She grabbed it held it to her ear and found Jill Wood was right beside her.

"Hallo," she said groggily into the phone, "who is it?"

"Just listen," said an unknown voice, "we have Hugo". At this point the sergeant leaned over and quietly turned the speaker phone on. In this way she would also be able to listen to the message coming through.

"He is not in any harm, but we are going to keep him until you deliver £3 million. We know you've got that kind of money. It was widely publicised that your father left you millions. If we don't get the money by next Friday afternoon, we'll tell you where to find your son's body!" The phone went dead.

Helen just sat there trembling violently. Who were they? How was she to get £3 million in less than a week? She knew they were right about her father's estate, but she didn't have access to £3 million just like that!

She sat there whimpering to herself. What could she do? How could she find out who these people were?

Jill put her arms round her, "It's alright Helen, we will find him."

"Did you hear what he said?"

"Yes. Would you be able to dial 1471 to see if a number was recorded?".

Helen picked up the phone again, before turning to the sergeant, "No, caller withheld the number".

"I'll get on to the Inspector and ask him to work on tracing the caller's number". The inspector answered immediately.

"Hello sergeant. Is Mrs Brierly with you? It sounds as though there have been some developments".

"Yes".

"What's happened?", asked the inspector.

Jill told him and heard an expletive followed by 'the bastard!"

"Look I'll be on my way back immediately. I am sorry I left, but there were some things I needed to put into place – like the border checks, just in case the kidnapper is still in the country. After a call like that she could well go into shock. Ask her for her doctor's number in the village. I'll get him to come over immediately and make sure she is holding up. When I get back to you we can discuss what the best thing is to do next. In the meantime, could you please write down exactly what was said; the time the call came through and anything else, any impression you or she might have got? Age; accent; anything odd you might have noticed. Also the names of anyone who might have a grudge against her and the names of anyone who knew she would be at her father's home this week. Take it easy with her. Please could you begin as soon I hang up. Now could I speak to Helen – ask her if she feels up to it."

The sergeant handed the phone over to Helen, "The inspector wants a word".

Upon gently enquiring if she was able to talk.

He heard her answer "yes" in a choking voice.

"Now Helen, please believe me, if they think your son is worth £3 million they are going to hang on for a few days and make sure he's kept safe. Take care of yourself and do try and get some rest – you are going to need to conserve your strength for the next few days," and with that he hung up.

The inspector and Rory arrived back at the manor about the same time and told Rory the gist of his conversation with Helen. "Well at least things are beginning to move," he said.

Rory was shocked by the demand being made by the kidnappers. "I know Helen is a very wealthy women, but how she is going to find that kind of money in less than a week, God only knows!"

Back at her father's former house, and sitting at his desk, Helen found a notepad in the desk and began to make notes. London accent, I think, she wrote. Slightly gruff voice – could be a disguise – but perhaps a smoker. Strangely the voice had reminded her a little of James, although she knew it wasn't him – maybe it was the way he said 'Hugo' with the emphasis on the first part of the name as in 'Hugh' with the 'go' fading away. It was strange because Hugo himself didn't pronounce it that way – he just said his name in a balanced way.

She had just begun to make the notes when the door quietly opened and the sergeant, who had exited herself while Helen spoke to the 'gov' entered.

"Are you alright?"

Helen shook her head and immediately told her about her call to the inspector.

"I have spoken to him. He's on his way here right now. I guess it will take him an hour or so, less probably in that fancy blue light flashing car! If those are notes you jotting down, please keep going and the guv has asked me to do the same. Do you fancy a cup of tea or coffee, or something stronger from your father's drinks cabinet?"

"Not now, thanks."

Helen began to put her thoughts down on paper. The phone call must have come through at about ten minutes to midnight, she thought. I'll check that with Jill because she was sitting beside me. Then I just sat there for a minute or two because I was so stunned.

She couldn't think of anyone who might have had a grudge against her, except James perhaps – but surely she had dealt with that situation?

Lots of people knew she would be in Sussex at her father's former manor house. She had been coming at this time of the year for at least 10 years, since she took over the organising of the big charity garden party Well James again, and of course the people at her office, particularly her young assistant. He had been very involved in arranging for the fair and the rides to take part in the annual event again.

He had actually organised many of the events taking place in the gardens and grounds of the house for her. But no, she couldn't believe he could be involved – there was no reason and besides he had been with her since her father's death three years before – she felt she knew everything about him. However she wrote down James Brierly, Jonathon Hayes, her P.A. and the names of other people at her office. She couldn't think of anyone else, except family and knew they wouldn't have done anything like this.

Sitting looking out of the window, the full moon lit up the shapes of the fairground and rides. The firm would be coming in the morning to collect everything – and, I imagine to be questioned by the police about what they might have seen. The big marquee stood out on the lawn with the colourful lights hung round the sides and roof. Helen thought, wearily – someone must have forgotten to switch them off. Oh well, it didn't matter. Tears began to roll down her cheeks again as she worried about Hugo and where he might be.

Chapter 7

The sergeant had found Helen's bed and bathroom, where she retrieved a fluffy dressing gown and persuaded Helen to put it on over her other clothes. The sergeant had noticed Helen shaking. The kind policewoman had decided to raid the drinks cabinet and handed her a large brandy.

"Drink this Helen, it will warm you up".

"Do you want anything?"

The sergeant giggled and replied, "No thank you. I am on duty and the inspector would arrest me for not following correct procedures. One day when all of this is over, and I am not on duty, I would love to join you".

Helen gratefully put the robe on and sipped at the brandy. The sergeant was right, she did feel less trembly. She sat in her father's special armchair and thought back about her life with James. She had only told the inspector part of it. Now she was ready to open up a bit more.

"My father set James up in business as a graphic designer and advertising agent because I had egged him on to do it. James leased an office in the Docklands area. It had large picture windows, which James said were necessary for the light. My father had suggested an office in Salisbury but James insisted on opening one in London – 'because that's where big business comes from.' James spent a fortune, my father's, on décor and furniture. 'You have to look successful in order to become successful' he kept saying to me"

He began well in his touting for business. He travelled backwards and forwards to London by train each day, sometimes not getting home until around 10.00 pm at night. Then came the evening when James phoned and said he had to stay in town overnight – something to do with taking an important client out for dinner. Helen wondered about clean clothes for the next day, but James told her he'd dashed into Marks and Spencer and bought a shirt and some underwear and socks. It wasn't until later, when she was going to bed that Helen noticed his toothbrush and razor were not in their usual places. Funny! He must have had a premonition and taken them with him.

She forgot about it until a couple of days later when he casually said he would probably stay up in London again. Helen mentioned the odd fact of his missing toothbrush and razor, but he denied it, said she must have been dreaming. Helen shrugged her shoulders and agreed, but she didn't think she was wrong.

Helen and James agreed to delay starting a family for a while. However as things often happen, she found she was pregnant. She was rather shocked, but being practical she settled down to plan how she would cope. Helen became busier, travelling with and on behalf of her father, to and from the United States. She went on book tours and then spent time in Hollywood talking to Directors and screenplay writers when they decided to adapt one of her father's stories into a film. She travelled with both her parents to Australia, South Africa and the Far East promoting the books for the publishers. As the months went by she knew she knew have to cut down and spend more time working from home.

Hugo arrived and Helen took him with her. The nanny often travelled as well. Then the next shock, she found she was expecting again. Later she wondered if James had deliberately caused this to happen. Some of her birth control pills seemed to be missing, but as a full time mum, and all the work for her father, she put it down to forgetfulness. Her mother became very much part of their life in helping out with the children

During this time James found a flat in London, it made more sense, he said, not to travel backwards and forwards every day, as it was very tiring and not much point in going down to Salisbury each night when Helen was away so much. He came down at weekends and they had lovely dinner parties with friends and did things like 'Glorious Goodwood', Ascot, and Cowes week. James had taken up sailing and become very keen.

Helen was too busy with children and the pressures of working with her father to really notice that their lovemaking had deteriorated. She just thought that having been married for several years they were becoming an 'old married couple'.

She remembered the exact time when she knew that James was having an affair.

One weekend James had said he wouldn't be able to get down the following weekend – he needed to stay in London. Helen immediately agreed that it was fine, instead of him coming to her, she would come up to London, do some shopping and perhaps they could go to the theatre.

James wriggled and squirmed. "Oh no, you would be on your own. I'm so busy with work that I wouldn't have time to entertain you," – and so on. Helen insisted. She didn't mind going shopping on her own, and not to worry, she would phone up an American friend who lived in London and they would go out to dinner together and catch up on all the gossip.

James said – "Yes, but I might be out very late. What about making it another weekend when I could devote myself to you? That would be much more fun, wouldn't it?"

"No," replied Helen, "I actually do want to come up next weekend. I'll come up on Friday morning, go and see Daddy's publisher and then come to the flat about 5.00pm."

James sulkily said, "Oh, alright then, if you must!"

Helen was a little surprised but felt that perhaps it was all her fault. She had, after all, travelled the world while poor James had been left behind working hard in England.

On the Friday she had done exactly what she'd said she would. She caught the 9.00am train from Salisbury and sat in 1st class working on the plans for a book launch taking place in Edinburgh in three weeks' time. She hoped she would be able to meet up with Sally McLeod there, if Sally could get away from the hotel and the two children she then had. I've seen so little of Sally since the time of her wedding and the pre-wedding party when I met James, reminisced Helen.

Helen got out at Waterloo and grabbed a taxi. She went straight to the Italian restaurant off Sloane Square where she had agreed to meet up with Marcia Holding, her father's publisher. Marcia was an American now living permanently in London. She said she loved the hustle and bustle of the City. She preferred London to Paris – "because at least the British speak the same language – sort of. I am no good at editing books though, because I can't *spell* the language!" Marcia always used to tease Helen that Americans were much more logical when it came to spelling!

Helen and Marcia were roughly the same age. Marcia hadn't married – yet! She said that men complicate life. Not that she didn't care for them, in some ways she cared too much. She was always dating and having affairs, but she didn't want to have them on a permanent basis cluttering up her charming small apartment.

Helen was already seated when Marcia arrived. It was still early and so few of the tables were occupied. The two women embraced and agreed that it was indeed great to meet up again. They both ordered martinis, which Marcia laughingly said should be six parts vodka and the martini bottle just waved over the top. Dry, ice-cold and a twist of lime.

"Perfect," murmured Helen.

"That's why I come here," replied Marcia. "The food is great - and they make a fantastic martini."

The two women ordered lunch and began to chat. Helen told her how odd James had been about the weekend.

"Ah," said Marcia. "I have heard some rumours and because he's your husband I have listened – and made some discreet enquiries. Do you know about his gambling?" When Helen shook her head, Marcia said, "No, I didn't think you did. I understand that he has dropped quite a packet recently at the tables, and that his business can't afford it."

Helen replied, "I know he's seems a bit subdued at the moment, but just put it down to his working too hard."

"Playing too hard!" Marcia didn't try to keep the sarcasm out of her voice.

"What else is there? Is there anything else I should know?"

"No." Marcia replied slowly. "Just keep an open mind. Don't let James pull the wool over your eyes, that's all."

The fun seemed to have gone out of the lunch. The two women completed their business and said goodbye. Helen went over to James's apartment. It was earlier than she had intended because normally she and Marcia sat and talked over lunch, drinking numerous cups of coffee.

When Helen arrived at the apartment block where James had his flat, she walked up the stairs to the second floor. She was about to knock on the door when she heard voices inside. James sounded agitated.

"No, you've got to go. My wife will be here about 5.00pm. You've got to collect your things together and leave right now."

A woman's voice answered, but Helen could not make out what was being said.

"I know you say you haven't anywhere to go Jodi, but I told you on Monday that you would have to make other arrangements for the weekend." James was raising his voice – almost panicking. "Look, I'll help you pack. Where's your small case? I'll collect your things out of the bathroom for you."

Again a woman's voice and then Helen heard James again. "I'll give you some money for a hotel. I'll call you tomorrow morning on your mobile when Helen is in the shower or something. You can come back on Sunday evening, so it's only for two nights after all."

Helen stood there trembling. Shock at what she had heard made her feel numb. How long had it been going on for, she wondered. Was it his first affair? Had it started as long ago as when James lied about taking his toothbrush and razor? Was this why they didn't make love anymore?

She stood there wondering what to do. Go in and confront them? Knock on the door and see James's shocked face? No, she thought, my pride won't let me act like a fishwife in front of that woman! She desperately wanted to see this 'Jodi' though. Was it someone she had met at some time? Was she younger and prettier than Helen was?

What would my father say I should do? she asked herself. He would tell me to walk away, think it through, and then try to discuss it in a reasonable way. If I burst in now I will certainly say something that would finish our marriage completely. Perhaps James has a good explanation. Unlikely though!

Helen dragged herself away from the door. She had come up the stairs feeling fairly positive, ready to try and talk to James – even about his gambling, if that was true. Helen stumbled back down to the street. Miraculously she got a taxi quickly.

"Waterloo Station, please," she told the driver. Normally she would have chatted to the cab driver, but tonight she was silent – deep in her thoughts.

"Got problems Miss?" asked the cabby.

"Yes," she replied in a daze.

"Here you are, Waterloo Station."

"Thank you," she said as she handed him a £20 note – she had nothing smaller.

"Your change Miss," offered the cabby.

"No, it's OK. You keep it."

In a dream she bought a ticket. In a dream she found a seat. The only tiny bit of amusement she found was that James had probably managed to get rid of that woman and was waiting for her to turn up. The lying cheat! Well she wasn't going to turn up and she wasn't going to phone him to tell him either. Let him sweat! She wouldn't even go home. She would go to her parent's house. She needed – really needed, to talk to her parents.

She thought she knew everything about James but that was the beginning. It was going to get worse, far worse!

Now, with all the pain of Hugo's kidnap while lying in her father's armchair, Helen thought again of Hugo. Where was *he?* In sheer exhaustion she fell asleep, feeling all the pain and anger that she had felt on that evening so many years ago. She thought the pain had gone away with time, but she was surprised that it hadn't. It still hurt.

Chapter 8

In the early hours of the morning the inspector stepped quietly into the room where the sergeant was sitting. She held a finger to her mouth to indicate the need for quietness.

"Did the doctor come?"

Jill nodded. "He gave her a mild sedative and on top of the brandy I had administered, she was asleep on the couch in no time".

"Great. Anything else happened?"

"No, nothing. Don't expect much now until the morning. How did you get on?"

"Just waiting for the bastard to do something else – and he will. I am assuming it is a he", replied the inspector.

"I have been going through the notes I've collected from people who are still here. Not much. Nobody saw anything suspicious. There must have been something! I guess it was so busy and everyone rushing to their favourite rides or stalls and one small boy wandering around, probably everyone thought he was with his family, and he wouldn't have looked disturbed or worried because he knows his way round".

"Right, sergeant, there's a couple of big comfortable looking sofas in the room across the hall, go and get your head down for a few hours – orders!"

Jill gratefully did as he told her, and like Helen was asleep in minutes.

Colin put his elbows on the table in front of him and held his head between his hands. To be honest he didn't know what to do. Until they got some kind of breakthrough there was nothing much anyone could do. He wanted to make a statement to the press, but what could he tell them? A child has been kidnapped and I don't who took him and I have no idea where he might be. So it was pointless to even think about saying anything. He had told Helen the child would be OK, but was he right? He was a copper, but right now he wasn't sure he was in the right job.

Shortly after, Alison crept into the room carrying a tray of tea. Seeing the inspector alone she said, "I wasn't sure if you were back. I've brought some tea, I thought Jill might be glad of it".

"I've sent her to get a few hours rest, but I'd love a cup. Please come and join me, I could do with some company. Have you seen Rory?"

"Yes, he's getting a couple of hours sleep, but we had a brief chat. If it is alright with you, I'd like to take the children back home, including Amy. I think they will be better off out of here. Also, we think we ought to look as though we are doing something about the ransom. I am planning to see our accountant and financial adviser this morning. I know there is not a lot we can do to get the money, but we can at least make some progress".

"Yes to both suggestions. When Helen is up to it, we need to get her on to her accountant".

"We think the simplest thing would be to take out a loan against our house. I think we could arrange that quite quickly".

The inspector said, "I've been going through the police statements. Looking at yours, is there anything else you can think of?"

"Only, did the kidnapper come prepared with some other clothes for Hugo? I don't believe he would go off without his shirt".

"Neither do I. We can try asking if anyone has seen a small boy – but then we have no idea who might have taken him and what he was dressed in".

"I think, I may have. Looking back, I think it is possible Hugo was sitting talking to an older man. He was sitting eating a burger and chatting. Don't ask me what the man looked like, they both had their backs to me. It was at a moment when I was distracted by the children".

"Where was this?"

"On a bench out towards the tennis court. They both had their backs to me – but what is curious is that it wasn't far from where Hugo's t-shirt was found".

"Thank you Alison, so maybe we can narrow down our search a bit. An older man. Anything else about him?"

Maybe grey hair, under a baseball cap. Nothing else – perhaps nondescript clothes – nothing flashy. I think that might be Rory about to leave, I'll just go and say goodbye".

Chapter 9

ernard settled himself down on his brother's sofa. He was not comfortable because he was a well-built man and sofa was not made for someone of his size. As he lay there he began thinking about what Keith had said about James and what a conniving little bastard he was. Bernard hadn't liked the comment about himself being 'thick' but he sort of accepted it. James had led both his half- brothers into dangerous situations, and from what Keith had implied, this was another when James would wriggle himself out of any responsibilities and leave Bernard to bear the brunt – and perhaps prison. Bernard didn't want that to happen so he lay there thinking of a way out.

First of all he'd decided not to take Hugo to France, because James was bound to pull a fast one. In fact, he thought he would go in the opposite direction, somewhere nobody would think about. He knew exactly where he would go - to an old cottage hidden away on a farm in Wales, but first of all, he decided a change of vehicle was vital. He couldn't be sure that no-one had seen him and Hugo in the white van.

Bernard slept fitfully and was up around 6.30am – too early to make arrangements for the hire of a car, instead he talked to his brother about his trip to visit James. How long it would take and how long he might have to wait for a ferry. Keith wasn't totally convinced but thought the sooner Hugo was out of his house the better, for himself and Janet and her kids.

Hugo came down with his new cousins, and while he was a bit tearful and asking for his mum, was satisfied when Bernard reassured him he would be seeing her soon.

After breakfast, Keith saw them off and Bernard headed for an Enterprise Car Hire place a couple of miles away. Leaving Hugo sitting the in car – he didn't want to the boy to burst out with anything that might cause the slightest suspicion, he headed inside.

Bernard checked his wallet for his driving license, and having found a utility bill in the van with his home address on, he pushed the door open and made for the reception area.. He knew that giving his home address was a bit risky, but he hadn't any options.

Choosing a silver/grey estate vehicle and paying in cash – he'd had to show a credit card, but wasn't planning on their using it, he collected the keys to go round to the parking area at the back of the building to collect the car and Hugo, saying as he went, "By the way mate, it's alright to leave my van here isn't it? I'm heading north and the old van is a bit dodgy these days and I don't want a breakdown".

"There's plenty of room, just park it in a corner out of the way".

"Thanks mate, see you next week". With a wave, he made his way to the rear of the building to Hugo was patiently sitting.

"Right Hugo, first we are going to see your dad, and then it is off to find your mum. You settle down, it won't be long".

They stopped at a petrol station to fill the car, and then headed towards a huge super-market.

"Why are we coming in here", asked Hugo.

"Your mum has gone to stay in a cottage. She's so tired after the fair, she says she needs some rest. So she's asked me to do some shopping for her and we'll take it with us. So as we go round, you pick out the things you like". Bernard knew he'd have to be careful about Hugo's choices as they were not going anywhere near a proper kitchen. So it would have to be mostly canned goods, with ring top pulls, biscuits, bread and food that could be made into sandwiches - at the last moment, he remembered toilet rolls.

Bernard noticed a couple of blow up mattresses and duvets and added them. Hugo didn't notice because Uncle Bernard had told him to choose a special toy to play with. Hugo chose a type of Gameboy, saying, "Mum won't let me have one of these".

Bernard had another idea, maybe he should get another phone, as he wasn't sure if the one he'd used to call Helen could be traced. He'd already noticed a dump truck which looked as though it was full of household waste in which he could discard his old phone. In the end he forgot to throw it away and when it was found in the boot of the car much later, it incriminated both he and James. What was even better was that with a new phone and number, nobody would be able to get hold of him – especially his brother and James, his half-brother! Before he left the store he visited the cash machine and took out the maximum he could for that day. Better to pay in cash.

Bernard, smiling to himself that he had duped everybody, headed for the M4 and Wales. Nobody was going to treat him like an idiot. After all, he'd known James all his life and believed he could control him!

As he headed further away from the south of England, he remembered what Keith had said about James – that he was a psychopath. Thinking about it, he knew Keith was right. Bernard remembered a time when James was aged four. Bernard and his mother had gone into their sitting room to find James standing on a chair, holding the little fish net, with which he'd scooped a lot of the fish out of the aquarium and dropped them on the table, where they were squirming around, gasping for air.

"Look mum, they're dancing!"

His mother grabbed the net, while pushing James on to the floor, before rescuing the fish and sliding them back into the water. It wasn't the first time James had done this, usually only one poor creature had been pulled out. This time there were a dozen or more. James had been told time and again to leave them alone. On this occasion, when all the fish were back in the aquarium, some not looking too bright. Bernard's mother picked James up and really smacked him as hard as she could. Most children would have cried out at the treatment – but not James. The look he gave his mother was one of pure hatred.

Thinking about this, Bernard knew he was doing the right thing by not taking Hugo to France. He really liked the little boy and delivering him into his father's hands would be inviting James to do something really bad.

While driving along, he vaguely wondered whether the flowers, and their demanding note had been delivered, congratulating himself for making sure he'd given nothing away – but he had, although he didn't know it then – the florist had as they always did, attach one of their business cards to the paper wrapping.

Chapter 10

elen woke up to see Alison standing near her with a cup of hot black coffee. "Thought you might need this, Sis. Would you like something to eat?"

Helen shook her head. "No, thank you, I couldn't eat".

"You've had almost nothing since breakfast yesterday".

Alison just shook her head again".

"I've been talking to Colin, the inspector. We've agreed that I should go home, taking my kids and Amy. I'll get my nanny to come and look after them – so they will be OK. Also, Rory and I have been talking about the money, we have to be practical and start making enquiries about raising the – money. Three million! Whew that's a lot".

"Yes, you're right. I'll see if I can talk to my accountant. Not now, perhaps later. Has Colin said anything about any news from the kidnapper?"

"No, nothing, and there's nothing he can do until they get a clue about who he, or they, are. He's having to wait. He says that sooner or later they will make a mistake".

"I hope it's sooner. I don't think I can stand much more!"

"Then I think I'll send you off to have a shower and a change of clothes".

People were out scouring the grounds for clues while others were being interviewed. The inspector felt so helpless. It was now a waiting game.

Helen slept fitfully and woke with a start just after 5.30 am. She thought she heard the children rustling around and then she remembered - how could she have gone to sleep when Hugo had been kidnapped? She began to torture herself wondering where he had been all night. Had he been frightened? Had they hurt him? Oh God, she thought, how will I ever live if he doesn't come back?

Helen suddenly remembered the newspaper. Her father had always had one delivered. She shot up of the sofa she had been sleeping in; she had to look, although she was terrified. What if the press had already found out? The kidnappers had threatened to kill Hugo if she told anyone – and she *had*. Alison and Rory knew and they had been persuaded her to call the police. What if someone at the police station had called the newspapers?

"Are you OK, Helen?" asked the sergeant.

"Not brilliant I'm afraid."

"I'm sure we'll get some feedback today. The gov should be here soon."

It was with considerable relief to both of them that the headlines proclaimed the stupidity of yet another Member of Parliament. Running off with the Foreign Secretary's wife wouldn't do his career any good! Helen scanned through page after page, but there were no articles saying that the grandson of Douglas Hugo Smith had been kidnapped.

Jill turned on the TV, while Helen snatched up the remote control, switching channels until she came to a news show.

"What if it was too late for the newspapers? Someone might still have leaked news to the TV programmes."

"I am sure they won't have done. With cases like this the police make sure that very few people know about what has happened."

Common sense and knowledge of the press told Helen they would have found a way to get in touch with her for her comments.

"Nothing so far on TV thank goodness", she said aloud.

The anguish she felt was awful. Were they going to keep contacting her every day? Were their demands going to get stronger? She didn't know if she could stay in control of her mind.

"Hugo, oh Hugo, when I find you I swear I'll never let you out of my sight ever again," she said aloud in despair.

Helen sat on her bed trembling; her vision blurred through the tears that sprang into her eyes. It was only sixteen hours since it happened but it felt like a lifetime – a nightmare of a lifetime!

Jill put her arms round Helen's shoulders and felt the convulsions running through her body. Dry sobs were wracking her whole being.

"It's all right Helen. We'll find Hugo. I'm sure we will and it could be the kidnappers are still in the area."

"I've got to do something. I can't just stay here waiting. I'll go mad if I do. Maybe he's lost or something. Maybe the kidnappers have let him go and he's still out there in the grounds!"

"Everything is under control at the moment. You just go and have a shower".

Helen had hardly been back downstairs again when there was a knock on the front door. The sergeant answered it and found a black car parked outside. The driver was holding a bouquet of flowers, with a small envelope saying 'Thankyou'.

"For Mrs Helen Brierly", asked the driver tentatively as he handed the flowers over.

Jill the sergeant, took them from his outstretched hand. "Thank you, I'll pass them on".

She closed the door behind him and made her way back to the study. Strange she thought, I don't feel comfortable about this at all. She pulled on a pair of surgical gloves.

"I think I will open the envelope Helen, if you don't mind. Got a nasty feeling about this".

Jill pulled out a small card with closely written words – *Start planning how you are going to get £3 million. You have until Friday afternoon at 4.30pm before we take action against the kid. We'll contact you again tomorrow to make sure you are co-operating. Make sure you DON'T contact the police.*

"I need to get in touch with the gov immediately. I'm sure he'll want to come over straight away. When he arrives, he'll decide what is best to do".

Helen went back into her father's study and sat down at his desk, while Jill got on the phone. It rang several times before a tired sounding Colin Jarvis answered.

"Hallo, Jarvis here."

"Hallo boss, they've struck again. This time it was a bunch of flowers. They were delivered about ten minutes ago by a local florist. The name of the florist is on a card attached to the flowers. Everything else is anonymous. Bet he didn't think of that – Maybe we can track him down this way?".

"Damn, damn, damn. What kind of bastards are we dealing with? But yes, this maybe the breakthrough we've been waiting for. How is she?"

"Very distraught, but she's holding up at the moment, well actually gov, I'm pretty worried, she seems to have gone from extreme anxiety to almost withdrawing into herself. She's sitting in a chair facing the window – not moving or reacting to anyone around her. Every now and again her lips move and I guess she's saying "Hugo", although no sound is coming out.

"I expect she's gone into shock. Can you get the doctor out again. I'll be there in fifteen minutes."

"Right, Sir. I'll have some coffee waiting for you".

"Thanks Sarg. But in the meantime – see if you can get Helen to drink a cup of hot, very sweet tea.".

Alison had come back into the room to say she was leaving shortly with her three and Amy. Jill told her about the bunch of flowers.

"Has the inspector been told about this?"

"Yes, he's on his way", replied Jill He seems to think this might be the breakthrough we've been waiting for".

"I hope to God it is", replied Alison, taking Jill to the other end of the room.

"Look, I don't believe she's in any shape to talk about raising the money at the moment. As soon as I can, I will speak to Rory. It is fortunate both Helen and I have the same accountant and financial guy. I think its best if I, or Rory and I, liaise with them shortly. Do you think it will be OK to explain what has happened. I will tell them the importance of keeping everything secret right now".

"The gov will be here very shortly and you can ask him, but I'm sure he'll say go ahead".

"Thanks Jill. Rory will still be heading for Maligny, near Chablis. This is where James has his French cottage. However, I'm sure he'll be able to talk briefly to me", Alison said as she left.

The inspector arrived and joined Helen and Jill in the study.

"OK sergeant let's have a look at the note. It's vicious and evil! But least we've got a clue. Have you seen anything of Detective Brown?"

"I think he's outside sir. Do you want me to find him?"

"Yes. Be as quick as you can. I want him to go and visit the florist".

Jill was lucky and found him just outside talking to a group who had been searching the grounds.

"Hey Tom, the governor wants you inside – immediately. He's in the study on the ground floor, I guess he's got a job for you.

The detective joined his boss.

"Take a seat for a moment Tom". The inspector filled him in with the history of the kidnap, and now the flowers.

"Get down there straight away and find out what happened. Get all the info you can. It could be the first link we have to the kidnapper.

The young detective headed out the door, jumped into his car and drove off for the nearby, small town. He only had to ask one woman for directions, and she sent him a little further along the high street.

Although it was a Bank Holiday, the shop was open and was busy, but Tom was lucky there were two people working. He enquired who was on duty on Saturday evening and was pointed in the direction of Pam, the younger one of the two.

"We are enquiring about some flowers your firm delivered to a Mrs Brierly this morning. What can you tell me about the order and the person who ordered them?".

Pam was very open and happy to open up, especially after she'd seen the policeman's badge.

"He was an old guy who came in late on Saturday. I was in the middle of closing. He really pissed me off. I had a date that evening and wanted to get away so I could have a bath, do my hair and get ready to go out! Then in he walks and wants to order some flowers for Monday morning. I asked him what message he wanted but just got – 'I've already written something. I'll put it in the envelope myself. He'd chosen one that said Thank You on the outside".

"What did he look like?"

"I don't know! I just wanted him to leave. I guess he probably had grey hair. I was pissed off as I just said. I had more plants and flowers to bring in from outside the shop, so I didn't pay much attention".

"How did he pay?"

"In cash. That pissed me off as well because I had to open the safe to put the money in. I'd already banked up for the day".

"So, what happened then?"

"He left and I went on with clearing up'"

"Did you see what happened to him?"

"Yeh, he crossed the road and got into a white van".

"Were there any markings on the van?"

"No, nothing, just a white van like lots of tradesmen drive".

"Did you happen to see the number plate?"

"No. I wasn't interested in him or his van, He just drove off. Is that all? My friend is struggling out there in the shop and I'd like to get back to my work".

"Sure. Before you go join her – please give me your details – name, home address, mobile number and email address to we can get in touch. You may be needed as a witness".

"Why? What the hell has he done?"

But the detective was already on his way to report back to the inspector. He hadn't got much out of Pam but hoped it would help in the search.

Chapter 11

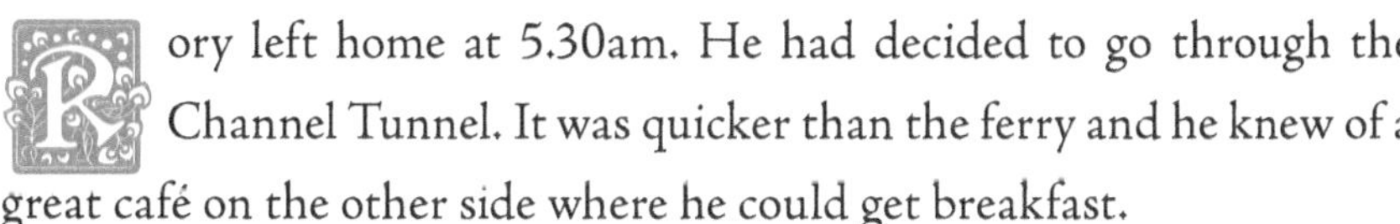

ory left home at 5.30am. He had decided to go through the Channel Tunnel. It was quicker than the ferry and he knew of a great café on the other side where he could get breakfast.

He was surprised to be directed to the priority queue and wondered if Colin had asked for this to happen, which enabled him to catch the next Eurostar. On the way to the tunnel, he'd stopped briefly to fill up his car and to buy some newspapers. Like Helen he was afraid the Press might have got hold of the story, and like Helen he was relieved to find nothing in any of them.

Once in France he joined the AutoRoute south via Reims to Troyes where he got off; on through Chaorce, where James's golf course was located and then through Tonnerre into Chablis where he stopped in the main square. After a salad and a beer in a little restaurant in the centre of the town, he picked up the phone and phoned James in the village of Maligny, just four miles north of Chablis.

He had worked out what to say on the road south. A client was holding a very big engagement party and wanted Chablis, red Burgundy and Champagne which he could get from his supplier in a village near Bar sur Seine, about fifty kilometres away.

"Hi, James," Rory said when the phone was answered.

"Rory, where are you?" asked James.

"I'm in Chablis. I'm over here on an emergency wine buying trip."

"Oh, you usually let me know when you're coming." Rory thought he sounded slightly panicky or at least uncomfortable - certainly not very pleased that Rory was only a few miles away. Why? Wondered Rory - a guilty conscience?

"I know but these people – their daughter just got engaged and they have ordered all sorts of wine from me. I didn't have enough in stock, and so I decided to come and get it myself. It's quicker than arranging to get it shipped from several suppliers. I'm coming to Maligny this afternoon. I always get my Premier and Grand Crus from the 'vigneron' on the main street. Thought I'd pop in and have a beer with you after I've been there."

"Where are you staying?" asked James, changing the subject.

"I thought I might check into the hotel in the middle of Chablis."

"Oh," said James; "you can have a bed here if you want one."

Rory's heart sank. Surely he can't have Hugo over here or he wouldn't be inviting me to stay, he thought to himself.

James interrupted his thoughts by asking a bit too casually perhaps, "Have you spoken to Helen recently?"

Rory thought he heard a sigh of relief when he answered, "No. I believe she's away on holiday at the moment, but she hasn't told us exactly where – somewhere on the coast I think."

"Right then, come on over when you've finished buying your Chablis," he said in a now cheerful voice.

Rory got into his car and drove alongside the river towards the village of Maligny. He always enjoyed looking at the vineyards stretching away up the hillside on the right hand side of the road. The perfect rows, now bushy and green in full leaf. He knew thick bunches of grapes hung among the leaves. They were hard to see because they were green as well. Another month and the owners would know whether the harvest was a good one or not. Most of the grapes were now picked by machine. Only the best grapes for the Grand Cru's were still carefully picked by hand.

He thought of the couple of times he had been over here for the harvest and had joined the pickers at lunchtime. At twelve noon the village siren sounded out from the Mairie. The noise always started the village dogs barking like mad, but the noise of the siren was the signal for the workers to leave their vineyards and make their way back to the village where the owner's wives had been slaving away all morning preparing crudités; coq au vin; salad and fruit tarts, all washed down with last year's petit Chablis. Everybody cheerful and laughing, "It's a good harvest," they had said, "As good as '86 we think!"

Rory had jokingly offered to help with the mountain of washing up left behind by the thirty-two workers after they returned to the vineyards. The ladies, three wives and a couple of sisters-in-law laughed and thanked him but said they could manage and Rory had gone on his way.

He turned into the yard where he would go and buy his wine. The manager met him, shook him by the hand and promptly opened a bottle of Grand Cru. They enjoyed a glass or two while discussing how big the Chablis area was growing. "Great demand!" said M. Colbert the manager, "and now, what can I get for you?" Rory put in his order and agreed to come back in the morning to collect it. M. Colbert pressed a couple of bottles of Premier Cru into his hands. "Un petit Cadeau – just a small gift," he said. They shook hands again and Rory, after a brief visit to James's French neighbours, made his way along the narrow street to James's house. He felt convinced that Hugo was not there, but he still had this nagging feeling that James was involved – somehow.

James greeted Rory with a smile. "Come on in. Do you want some help with your bags?"

"No, I've only got a small one, thanks."

"I've put you in the downstairs bedroom, its cooler in there at this time of year. Oh, and by the way I want you to meet Christiane later.

She's off visiting an elderly aunt but will be back in about an hour and a half. Drop your bag off and I'll get us a drink. Whisky, OK?"

Rory put his bag in the downstairs bedroom, wondering who the hell Christiane was, before wandering outside to the patio area and joining James at the table there. On the way through the house he had looked for any signs of Hugo, but there were none.

They chatted for a while and then James said "Will you excuse me for a few minutes, I've just got to walk down to the Boulangerie for a baguette for dinner. Come with me if you like."

"No I won't, thank you. It's already been a long day. If you don't mind I'll just get myself another drink and sit here and relax for a few minutes."

"Sorry Rory, you sit there, I'll get you another drink. Scotch again?"

Rory nodded. Actually he wasn't that tired and would normally have enjoyed the short walk but he felt this might be his only opportunity to have a quick look round on his own.

As soon as James had gone down the street, Rory nipped into the house. Nothing downstairs, but he had already checked there. Upstairs he quickly checked the spare bedroom. Nothing. Twin beds neatly made up but nothing personal in that room. James's room next - double bed and, hanging on the back of the bathroom door, two dressing gowns, one man's and one that was definitely for a woman. Oh, oh, thought James, she's not just a dinner guest; she obviously spends the night here. For some reason it made him angry. He knew that James and Helen were going through a divorce, but somehow it made James seem disloyal to his wife. But James has always had other women on the side – I suppose he hasn't changed.

The only thing that caught Rory's attention was James's passport on the bedside table. Why would he leave that lying around? There was no point in looking in it for a date of entry into France – customs looked, sometimes, but didn't bother to stamp them anymore.

He could see nothing else of interest.

"Better get back down and outside again before James returns from his shopping" he said aloud to himself, and with that he went downstairs. When James returned he found Rory sitting just where he had left him, quietly sipping his whisky.

Later on that evening after dinner he, James and Christiane sat outside with brandies. Rory said to James, "As a matter of fact, I tried to call you a couple of times yesterday but got no reply. I just wanted to let you know I was coming over."

James turned round sharply and looked at Rory. He hurriedly said, "I was playing golf at Chaorce – I always play there on Saturdays."

"Did you play well?"

"Matter of fact, I came second. I had a good round. Would have won it if I hadn't lost my ball into the pond on the 17th."

They talked a little longer before Rory excused himself and went to bed. He thought about the brief conversation he'd had with Inspector Jarvis earlier on. Rory had made an excuse to go to his car while James and Christiane prepared dinner. The inspector told him about the flowers Helen had received that morning and Rory told the inspector of his disappointment at not finding Hugo. The inspector offered to call both Helen and Alison to let them know the situation and Rory gratefully agreed to his suggestion.

As Rory got ready for bed he thought he might just drop into the golf clubhouse at Chaorce on his way to get his champagne. James had boasted about the result yesterday. It would be easy to check. They put the results up on a big board in the entrance. If he really had played, then it would prove that he couldn't have been in England – but if he was lying, then Rory wanted to know why.

One odd thing had occurred during the evening. The phone had rung and James had rushed to answer it.

"Keith? Is anything wrong?" he heard James ask. "What! Where's he gone?" "You don't know – isn't he in London?" "Well try and find out and call me back as soon as possible" "No. No I don't think it's your fault." "OK, OK just call me when you can."

When James returned to the table and sat down he obviously felt he needed to make some kind of explanation. "That was just somebody who was sorting out an insurance problem for me. The fellow I've got a claim against has disappeared." He didn't sound very convincing – but perhaps Rory was just imagining that.

Something else to tell the inspector, thought James as he surreptitiously glanced at his watch to check the time of the call. Must make a note of what was said, and when, before I go to bed. I might need it as evidence later.

Next morning after breakfast Rory asked to use the phone. He called Madame Balmain. She and her husband owned some vineyards in another village near Chablis. The wine in this village was predominantly red and theirs was particularly good.

Yes she would be in at 11.00am this morning. She would be delighted to see M. Johnson again. "Au revoir, Monsieur – at 11.00 this morning."

Rory phoned his champagne supplier next who was very different from the last call. Madame Balmain was very nice but, where she was 'French village', Daniel was definitely from a 'well to do' family. Big house in a village near Bar sur Seine and another family home in Paris.

He would also be delighted to see Rory! Rory would have to be careful. Both Madame Balmain and Daniel Cardin would be very hospitable. He would certainly be expected to taste their delicious wines.

Rory had felt guilty about staying on in France and going about his business of wine importing. But Colin asked him to remain over there for the time being as they wanted Rory to keep an eye on James. Rory told him this was fine.

As soon as he had left James's after breakfast, he pulled into a lane off the main road and telephoned Inspector Jarvis. The inspector filled him in a little more about the previous day's proceedings.

"How's Helen?"

"Not good, but she's getting support from all of us. She's been carrying around the red shirt we found in the garden. It almost like a comfort blanket, something the Hugo had been wearing".

"No, that's not good, but still if it gives her comfort, she's better doing that. I am very worried about her".

"As we all are. We are hoping she will improve now we know we have some clues about the kidnapper".

Rory made his suggestion of checking at the Golf Club to see if James had actually played on Saturday when he'd claimed he'd come in second. Rory had played there with James in the past and knew the set-up. He also knew they kept a big book, a permanent record of everyone who had entered every competition. It would be easy to find out if James had been lying.

He also told the inspector about the mysterious phone call. No more than Rory, did the inspector believe that it had been a problem to do with insurance. He congratulated Rory and said "Right, we've got a name. Well done. When will you be back in England, Sir?"

"I plan to go into the village, pick up my Chablis and then I have arranged to be in Irancy at 11.00am. After that I'll be on my way to Chaorce where I'll check on the competition and grab a sandwich. From there it will only take about twenty minutes to where I get my champagne. As soon as I have completed the purchase, probably about 3.30pm French time, I'll be on my way back to Chablis where I'll check into a hotel. James rarely visits Chablis so I don't think there is much chance of him seeing me".

"Thank you for your help. I'll talk to you later. Good bye."

"Before you go Colin, how is Helen?"

Worried though he was about his sister-in-law, Rory felt a bit better as he drove off round the various wine stops he had to make. At 1.00pm he turned off the road and into the driveway to the golf course. As he turned into the main entrance he looked at the Chateau with pleasure. He always enjoyed driving in here. Going past the old Chateau from which the view of the course was now blocked by a much bigger building erected in the late 1800's. Turrets, high angled roofs and different coloured stone and brick made up what was now the clubhouse and apartments owned by wealthy Parisians, who came down at weekends.

It was Monday and so very few people were around. A few foreign cars and the odd one with Parisian number plates.

Rory climbed the steps and entered through the front door. He went straight over to the membership and competition boards. There was James's name on the membership list. He had himself once enquired about membership. It was incredibly expensive and it would have cost James a 'bomb' to join – or at least Helen a 'bomb' because she had been funding James for years.

He carefully checked and re-checked the competition lists. James had been lying – a Monsieur Roget had come in second. He went to the office where the competition book was kept and in which everyone had to sign before they could take part. The girl in the office recognised him, smiled and made no difficulty about him looking at the page for last Saturday. Nothing there - no sign of James having played.

He asked, "Were you here on Saturday?"

She nodded and said, "Oui Monsieur."

"Did my brother-in-law, M. Brierly play on Saturday?"

"Non. He was due to play with M. Patrick Claudet, but he telephoned on Thursday and said he had urgent business and please could we pair M. Claudet up with someone else. We haven't heard from him since, but he is expected to play this coming Saturday."

Rory said, "Merci" and went through the bar and out on to the patio where he could look out across the course. He ordered a beer and a baguette with ham in it and sat staring down the 1st fairway feeling extremely angry.

The lying bastard! said Rory to himself. I'm sure he's involved with the kidnapping of his own son. If he was here now I'd take a golf club to his head and when he was down I'd kick him so hard in the 'balls' that he would never be able to fuck another woman – ever!! "Bastard!" Rory was so angry he hadn't noticed that his last word 'bastard' had been said out loud. It was only when the girl behind the bar getting a beer for him said a startled "Monsieur?" that he realised.

"Pardon. I'm sorry. I wasn't speaking to you. I was thinking of something very bad."

The very bad was not only the kidnapping which Rory now believed could definitely be laid at James's door, but also the disclosures James had made last night when, after too many glasses of wine and brandy, he'd confided in Rory that Christiane had been around for years. "She and her old mother shared a house in the village. Mother retired to bed very early, and besides," said James laughing, "was stone deaf." Many a time when Helen remained at the cottage with Hugo, and then Hugo and Amy, instead of going to the Bar Tabac to meet up with some of the locals, he had stopped off at Christiane's house, where she entertained him in her comfortable bed. Mother was now dead and so it was more convenient for Christiane to move in with him. "Helen didn't want me," he slurred, "so what's a man supposed to do? Anyway, we're nearly divorced and Christiane understands me." It was at this point that Rory had retired to bed.

Rory finished his beer and baguette, paid and left. Sitting in his car before driving off, he began to wonder it James had come over to England and kidnapped his own son? It was possible, but if he had done, where the hell was Hugo now?

Rory considered whether to go back to Maligny and confront James with his findings at the Golf Club. He really felt an extreme urge to beat the man up! Rory regretfully decided not to. Much as he wanted to hit him he felt he should wait. Hitting James would only alert him to the fact they knew of his involvement in the kidnapping.

As Rory drove away he doubted whether he would ever come back to Chaorce to play golf.

It took him about twenty minutes to reach the village where he bought his champagne. What a contrast! His burgundy was bought in Irancy out of a building that was part garage, part wine cellar and part bottling store. The office where he did business with Daniel Cardin was opulent - marble floors and comfortable chairs. The very efficient secretary greeted him with a handshake and said she would call Daniel immediately. Daniel arrived with a bottle of chilled champagne and led him into another room where they sat down to enjoy a glass or two of the delicious ice-cold wine.

They chatted for a while. Daniel told him about his recent holiday in Scotland when it rained every day and Rory told him about his family's visit to Euro Disney and how much they had enjoyed it.

Rory ordered the champagne he needed and while Daniel collected the cases, Rory paid and was delighted to receive his third gift for the trip - this time a very nice champagne ice bucket.

The two men shook hands again and Rory was on his way. He felt a little better. It was always nice to visit these people personally and he enjoyed speaking French. Now he was heading back to Chablis to see if he could find out anything else, and besides, the inspector wanted him to keep an eye on James. He had already spoken to Alison and agreed with her they should help out financially. He said he was happy to talk to the accountant and finance guy, but at the moment, Alison would have to get on with it herself.

Inspector Jarvis had told him, when he phoned to report his findings at the golf club, that Alison had returned to the manor house, after a visit to their joint accountant, and was sharing the duty of looking after Helen. Everyone, except Helen, felt she needed someone close by at all times. Colin told him about the police statement they would be releasing to the press in about half an hour.

"I won't be there. I have briefed the Superintendent myself. I don't want my name or picture on TV or in the papers".

What will he be saying?"

"Simply that the kidnap of a child has happened and the police are looking for an older, grey haired man, with a small boy with him. We need to ask the public to be aware and keep a lookout".

"You're asking for trouble, aren't you? You'll get thousands of calls from cranks or well-intentioned people calling in!"

"I know, but we have to do it on the off chance somebody calls in who does know something!"

"Let me know how it goes. I assume you are not telling Helen".

"No, Alison or Jill will distract her somehow, and besides, she is not ready for any more pressure. She's had a mild sedative from her doctor and is resting at the moment, and the tomorrow's newspaper will have mysteriously not been delivered. I am hoping something will come out of the press release and we can give her some positive information".

"I'm on my way back to Chablis. I have spoken to James's French next door neighbour, she thought the world of Helen and the children, but hates him. She and her husband are going to keep an eye on James and will call me if he goes off in his car".

"Good. Keep me posted".

Chapter 12

At a little before 10.45am, after the shopping and filling up the car, Uncle Bernard and Hugo set off. At first Hugo was quite relaxed. He was going back to his mum and although he hadn't enjoyed being taken away from her, he'd met some really nice cousins he hadn't known existed. He hoped his mum would let him go on visiting them. They were going to watch a James Bond film, and Michael had said there were some really cool rock pools with crabs and things that he would take Hugo to see.

After driving for about fifteen minutes Hugo asked, "When are we going to get there Uncle Bernard?"

"Soon son," was the reply.

After about an hour Hugo realised something was wrong. They were well out of the town and were about to join the motorway.

"Where are we going?"

"Your mum's gone home. We're going there."

"Why didn't she come and get me then?"

"She asked me to take you to her," lied Uncle Bernard.

Time went by. Hugo had eaten some biscuits and drunk a can of Coke. He didn't think it took this long to get to his home, but he had been engrossed in the game Uncle Bernard had bought for him. Suddenly they were driving through country lanes, and Hugo noticed the road signs were in English and another language.

"Where are we?"

"We're in Wales, son".

"Why? I want to go home".

"You are I are going camping for a few days".

Hugo began to cry, "But I don't want to go camping – I want to go home!"

Back in the car Hugo dozed off. He didn't mean to but it was warm and he couldn't stop himself going to sleep. When he jerked awake some hours later, it was late afternoon. Uncle Bernard was just filling up the car with petrol. He paid and they were off again.

"Where are we going?"

"You and I are going camping for a few days, son."

Hugo began to cry, "I want my mum……"

"Shut up. If your mum does as I ask, you'll be back with her on Friday."

"But I want her now!" he wailed.

Uncle Bernard just turned up the radio and ignored him.

They had taken a cross country route and so it was late afternoon when they turned into what seemed to be a deserted farmyard. There wasn't a farmhouse, just old buildings with the half doors hanging open. Uncle Bernard drove his car into one of the buildings – an old hay barn, and began to collect things from the boot.

"My dad brought my mother and me here to stay near here when I was little," said Uncle Bernard. "I don't remember that visit, but a few years later, after dad had left us, my mum brought Keith and me back to stay with the farmer and his wife. I've never forgotten that holiday," - but he hoped everyone else had, especially Keith. He didn't trust Keith. Keith had always been soft, just like his father, he thought cynically.

Bernard knew the old buildings still existed. He had visited the area the previous year out of curiosity. He'd been a bit shocked at the disrepair the cottage had fallen into, but now believed it suited his purpose beautifully – nobody would think of looking for them in such a tumbledown place. As he looked around he noticed the old dead tree still standing behind the cottage. It had been struck by lightning at the time he, his mother and Keith were staying with Dai Morgan, the farmer who owned the land where the cottage was. He remembered how frightened he had been when the storm broke out overhead. There had been one huge flash and the sound of thunder came immediately after and hearing the farmer say that close by had surely been struck had really scared him.

Between them they carried some of the stuff from the car to the old cottage some one hundred yards away. Hugo was appalled when he saw where they would be staying, but all Uncle Bernard said was, "Not as good as it was, but I think we can camp out here OK for a few days."

They made three trips to the car before collecting all the food and camping gear they needed. Hugo kept whimpering because he was cold and hungry and a bit scared. Surely Uncle Bernard wouldn't hurt him otherwise why would his dad have left him with him. He hated the cottage. It was dirty and there was no electricity or anything. There were piles of wood everywhere. Why would anyone put wood in the bedrooms, he wondered.

His uncle got out the portable barbecue he'd also bought at the supermarket and cooked some hotdogs he'd got out of a tin for Hugo, and some sort of meat for himself. Hugo enjoyed barbecues so he was happy. There was nothing to sit on while they ate their meal and Uncle Bernard muttered he wished he'd thought of buying two folding chairs and a picnic table. He did manage to find a couple of plastic plates stashed away among some camping gear. However, down by the stream, a huge branch had fallen off an ancient oak tree and they sat side by side on it to eat their supper.

After eating Uncle Bernard washed their plates in the stream. Hugo said "Ugh!" but Uncle Bernard replied that the water came from a spring a little way away in the field and so the water was absolutely pure and clean. "I'll show you where it is later," he said.

Returning to the cottage, his uncle began removing some of the wood from what would have been the sitting room/kitchen in former days. As he did so he mumbled to himself – I wonder who piled all this stuff into these rooms. Still it'll come in handy if I can get the old iron stove to work.

He had clambered up the very steep, narrow staircase to check out the two bedrooms soon after they arrived, but they were even fuller with sticks and branches – all absolutely bone dry. Must have been here for years, he thought.

Downstairs he cleared a space big enough for them both to lie down to sleep for the night, while managing to drag some of the wood into the kitchen and throw the rest out through the front door. It had taken him some considerable time to work the door and windows open as they were so warped with age. The hinges were also rusted and very stiff. In the end Bernard had given up trying to open one of the windows and had simply broken the glass instead to get a bit of fresh air into the room.

"Place is falling down, won't make much difference as it's almost a ruin already." He did go round and pick up most of the pieces of glass. "Don't want any animals cutting their feet," he told Hugo.

By the time they'd cleared the wood, and shared some chocolate and biscuits, Uncle Bernard had found an old yard brush in one of the barns to sweep the cottage out a bit, dusk was beginning to fall. Bernard got out two inflatable mattresses and the foot pump he'd bought in the supermarket and pumped up their temporary beds. He invited Hugo to choose which one he wanted and left the room to let Hugo settle down to sob himself to sleep.

Hugo lay there crying for his mum and wishing he could just say hallo to her. He'd looked round for a telephone soon after they'd got there believing that all houses had phones, but of course, because of the remoteness of the cottage, it had never had a telephone. Anyway, Hugo thought to himself, I can't tell mum where I am because I don't know! - and his sobbing increased in volume.

Bernard stood outside listening to Hugo's crying and quietly switched on the tape recorder he'd had brought from his van. He couldn't remember why it had been there, but the idea came to him that he might use it to put even more pressure on Helen to cough up the money. Just listening to her son's unhappiness should do the trick! Later, when he played the recording during his last demand for money, Alison who was pretending to be Helen, did begin to cry and say to herself, thank God it was me and not Helen he thought he was talking because it would certainly have pushed her over the edge. The sheer cruelty was beyond Alison's comprehension.

Hugo eventually dozed off and Bernard went back outside to sit on the branch of the old oak tree again. Sitting there quietly puffing away on his pipe, he began to think back over his life again up until the present moment.

Bernard was not a genuinely bad man, but he had been greatly influenced, first by his mother and then, much later, after she had remarried, and James had been born and grown up, by him too.

It was only when he got older he learnt about the marriage between such an unequal pair. it. At the time her own family discovered she was pregnant, her family initially vowed to disown her. In those days girls were not supposed to get pregnant before they got married, but her Methodist God-fearing father and stepped in and forced the pair to the altar.

After his father, Douglas Hugo Smith had left, there was never a day when his mother hadn't moaned on about it. He looked back and thought that bringing up two boys on her own during the thirties. She'd worked very hard to earn enough money to keep the three of them in food and clothes – sometimes doing two different jobs. He was very young when the split came and he never thought about how much it had been his mother's fault for the breakup of the marriage.

Rumours of a war were circulating in early 1939 when Bernard left school at the age of thirteen. He was a big strapping lad who looked older than he actually was. His first job was on the docks down at Tilbury. There he did all sorts of jobs around the berths of the passenger liners, which departed regularly for different parts of the world. Perhaps this was where it started, his love of the sea and the longing to travel. Later on, after the war, when he went back to work at Tilbury, envy began to creep into his life. Seeing the wealthy passengers dressed in their finery, going on board with their expensive luggage, heading for their luxurious cabins to journey off to India and the Far East had made him long to be able to afford to copy them. His mum increased his feelings of jealousy with her perpetual nagging on about other people having more than they did. By now she began to read about her former husband and his growing wealth.

Bernard had been married briefly but it didn't last. His wife complained about her domineering mother-in-law and had called him 'mummy's boy'. He guessed she'd been right and they divorced acrimoniously without any children coming from their relationship. He then moved back in with his mum and step-father and little brother, James.

Over the years his mother became more and more twisted and, when, not long before she died, her former husband Douglas Smith had been knighted for services to his country, she became almost incoherent with her vitriol.

"I should have been 'Lady' Smith she'd screamed on more than one occasion". Nothing anyone could say would make her believe that, if the two of them had remained together, the likelihood of it happening was remote.

It was only during the war, when he'd finally been able to join the navy, that he'd felt really free. The war was nearly over when he was called up and so he wasn't in for very long, but he'd loved the companionship of the other men and he'd seen places in a world very foreign to a lad from the East End of London.

As the thoughts chased through his mind, he began to think about why he was hiding away in a remote cottage with a small boy and attempting to extort £3 million. It was James of course. James had led him into it. Blackmailed him more like! Many years before, Bernard made a very stupid mistake and James found out about it.

It had happened when one day Bernard was working at the docks, where he was by now a senior stevedore, he'd found a briefcase left lying in the corner of the customs shed. Upon opening it, he'd saw it contained about £20,000. His first reaction had been to turn it in and then his enviousness of those people who were richer than he was overwhelmed him. Ideas of his being able to go off on a cruise flooded into his mind. I could be one of them, he thought, someone would take my bags on to one of these beautiful ships. I could sail off to Hong Kong and Japan and other exotic places. His mind wandered on.

Nobody was around and, as far as he knew, nobody else had seen the briefcase. Bernard quickly grabbed the case and threw it into the empty container he was bringing back from discharging goods into the ship's hold. Driving the fork lift truck, he rounded a corner of a freight building and headed towards the car park where his 'pride and joy' was parked – a dark blue Ford Mondeo. There he simply removed the case and dropped it into the boot of his car. Nobody would think twice about asking why he was in the car park and what he was doing because he was senior enough for them to accept that he knew what he was up to. He did have a few bad moments when custom officials seemed to be searching for something in the customs shed, but it turned out they were just looking for some lost paperwork.

Later on he removed the cash and got rid of the briefcase. It went overboard, weighted down, into the sea from his small fishing boat, off Southend-on-Sea.

In one way he was fortunate that the owner didn't realise it was missing until the ship was two days out at sea because by then nobody at the docks knew anything about it. In another way he was unfortunate, although it was his own fault, James found out about the theft. Bernard had gone down to the local pub with James one evening where he had foolishly thrown a bit more money around than he should have done. After a few pints he also bragged about going on a cruise. The other chaps believed him when he said he'd won a packet on 'the dogs' – but James didn't. He knew Bernard was not a gambler. He bought Bernard a few more scotches and then wormed the information out of him. After that he never hesitated to scrounge off Bernard. 'Loans' he called them – but always with the threat of going to the police if Bernard faltered about giving him any more money. Bernard had given in to everything he asked – including helping him with the kidnap of Hugo!

Back in the present, Bernard got to his feet and slowly made his way back into the cottage.

"Thank goodness there's a bright moon tonight," he said out loud to himself. "At least I can see to find my mattress without falling over Hugo."

He had brought his pyjamas with him but decided not to bother getting into them. He lowered himself down onto the inflatable mattress still in his shirt and trousers, where he lay staring up at the ceiling, musing about his life. What a fool he'd been. Why hadn't he stayed married and had children like Keith? He probably would have grandchildren by now.

If he hadn't been forced to hide out with Hugo he would have enjoyed spending time with a little lad like him – teaching him how to fish and all the other things he had enjoyed when he'd been the same age as Hugo was now.

He'd never gone on the cruise either – James had seen to that! By the time James had gone through the £20,000 plus a great deal more, he couldn't afford to go. He lay there thinking. The mattress wasn't comfortable either and it was long into the night before he drifted off into a troubled sleep.

Chapter 13

t exactly 5.30pm on Monday afternoon the press release was delivered.

It read, *At some time during yesterday afternoon, a child of eight was kidnapped. All we have at the moment is the sighting of a white van in the south of England, which was seen on Saturday afternoon just before 5pm. We believe the driver of this van was involved in the kidnapping on the following day, Sunday. We are not issuing anything further for the sake of the child and the parents and family.*

Anyone who might know anything is asked to contact this number....

Journalists and TV people shouted questions about where it had taken place and what's the name of the child. All they got was, "Thank you ladies and gentlemen. I have no need to tell you the seriousness of the situation and ask that you do not attempt to pry into the case".

Reporters dashed off to their desks to prepare something for their papers next day, while film crews sent pictures of the interview – all of them aware they been given very little to go on.

As Rory had suggested, the phone was ringing off the wall. Everybody knew somebody with a white van and were anxious to help. Several psychics called to say they knew where the child was, but each one suggested different places, they were not taken seriously!

Unfortunately for the police the three people involved with the kidnapping didn't see the TV broadcast and only one of them read the news in the papers the following day.

One of them was in Wales, one in France and the third one at an away football match who didn't bother to turn on his TV that night after he got home.

The other witness contacted the police as soon as he reached the car hire firm premises. He told them about the man who'd come in to hire a car and who'd left the van parked in their parking lot at the rear of the building.

He added, "I was in the back room and noticed this older man park his van up and then help a little boy out of it and into our car".

"Do you have any details of who he was?"

"Yes, he gave us his name and address, and although he said he preferred to pay in cash, we insisted we took a copy of his bank card – so we've got all of these here".

"Did he tell you where he was going?"

"Nope, but I got the impression he was heading for the north east, maybe Newcastle way, or Scotland".

"Right. Don't let anyone go near the van. We'll have someone there as soon as we can".

The second result of the press release was to have a far greater impact on the case.

Although Keith didn't turn on his TV and see the news, his daughter Janet called him.

"Dad, we've got a problem. Bernard has been seen with his white van and the police are searching for him. What are we going to do?"

To begin with Keith didn't know what Janet was on about until she explained the press release. The he went quiet.

"Dad, are you still there? I said – what are we going to do?"

"I don't know. All I can think of is to call him and James. I am hoping Bernard has reached James in France and has handed Hugo over to him. Look I'll try them both and call you back".

But Keith didn't get a reply from either of them. James was probably drunk and it sounded as though Bernard's phone was either not charged or it had somehow stopped working. He called Janet back and told her the results of his efforts.

"You'd better think about what to do. There's not much we can do tonight. Try both of them early tomorrow morning. I'll get the kids to school and come straight on over. Good night Dad. We have to make some decisions – for the sake of Hugo and his mother".

Keith tried both brothers early on Tuesday morning. From Bernard he got nothing. With James it was, "What the hell are you calling this early for?"

"The police are searching for Bernard. They've had a tipoff about him being seen – at least his van has been seen. I just want to know if he has arrived at your cottage yet?"

"No he hasn't. And I've got Helen's brother-in-law here. Says he's on a wine buying trip. Have you tried calling Bernard to find out what the hell he's up to?"

"Yes, of course, but I'm not getting an answer".

"So what are you going to do?"

"Only thing I can do. Get in touch with the police and tell them all I know", replied Keith.

Suddenly James changed out of his sleepy mode and shouted back, "You can't do that. We'll all be in trouble, especially you Keith. I'll tell them you are the one behind all of this. I'll…."

Keith just hung up.

It was a pity Rory hadn't heard the call or he'd have learnt a lot more, as it was, James seemed to be very edgy. He even suggested that Rory call Helen to see how she was.

Janet arrived to find her dad with his head in his hands.

"I'll get us both a cup of tea".

Keith told her about his phone calls. Nothing from Bernard and James had turned nasty while threatening to blame him.

"Typical of James! Are you really going to contact the police?"

"Nothing else I can do. Just worried about you Jan, and the kids".

"Don't worry about us. I should think everybody, and their mother have been calling the number, so I've bought some papers this morning – they are not good reading I'm afraid. I think I'll drive you to the local police station, and I'm coming in with you".

"Not yet. Please just wait for a little longer in case Bernard has heard and is trying to call me".

Janet could see her father was in a terrible state and so she quietly asked him to tell her more about his family.

"Mum, your grandmother, and Douglas Smith met when they were very young and being very naive and inexperienced the pair of them got carried away and your grandmother became pregnant. In those days it wasn't done to be an unmarried mother, so as quickly as her parents could they made them get married, and Bernard was born".

Janet refilled her father's teacup and handed it to him.

Dad was a nice man, very creative and had always had a gift for writing. Mum was completely the opposite, nagging and blaming him for everything. Over the years I began to realise she was very manipulative. If she wanted to do something which she thought might be unpopular with other people, she invariably picked out the weakest in the group and got them on her side so that she could push through her ideas while telling everyone it was really their idea and that she'd gone along with them. Oh, she was clever, not in the intellectual way, more cunning. Dad was more of a dreamer. Anyway, he'd had enough and told her he wanted out of their marriage and that if she went along with a divorce he would support her and Bernard and I until we were old enough to leave school".

"I believe she'd already got James's dad, Albert Brierly, lined up, so she agreed. It took a while but the divorce did go through eventually and by this time James had been born. He was nasty from the day he was born and so was she. She even tried to blackmail dad and get more money out of him to pay for James, but dad wasn't having any of it and told her to get lost!"

Janet indicated they should go, but Keith wanted to continue to wait a little longer.

"The pair of them, mum and James, were cheating and conniving and mum encouraged him to become as spiteful as she was. By this time dad was a successful writer and we saw in the papers he had married again. Bernard and I were sad that we didn't see him any more – but he was always good to us".

"Anyway James somehow managed to meet Helen, dad's eldest daughter and persuaded her to marry him. Mum had died by then, but it still seems a bit strange that nobody from our family was invited to the wedding. As I never met dad again, I have always wondered if he knew James was his step-son".

"Dad, I think we ought to go to the police station now", said Janet gently.

"Yes, I've got to get it over, but it's going to be very hard to explain. It's you and the kids – I'm really worried about you and the kids and Jack, of course", said her father as he gave her a quick hug before they headed out for her car.

"Don't worry about us. I should think that everybody, and their mother have been calling the number, so I've bought some papers this morning they are not good reading, I'm afraid", she said as pulled out of her father's driveway.

Arriving at the police station, a dozy young man, as Janet later called him, came out of a back room to speak to them. When he heard what they'd come about, he told them they had better speak to the inspector. He was out now, but if they didn't mind waiting, he'd get on to him straight away. Janet and Keith *did* mind waiting and hoped it wouldn't be too long. It was nearly half an hour before he turned up.

As soon as he heard about why they had come, he told them he'd have to get on to the man in charge. That took another fifteen minutes before they were connected to Inspector Colin Jarvis.

"Right Sir, I need you to tell me what you know. We'll be taking a full statement from you, but as we are up against time, we'll start now."

It all poured out. How he had two brothers – one a full brother and the other a half-brother, James. It was James who'd planned it all, and in Keith's opinion, was a nasty piece of work who'd stop at nothing to get his own way.

"James was blackmailing Helen, the mother, demanding £3 million from her for the return of Hugo". Keith didn't notice it, but unseen the inspector straightened his back. This one was for real. Nothing had been said about how much money was being demanded, or the name of the child.

Inspector Jarvis decided to change tack. He'd been a bit surprised when Keith told him his surname was Smith.

"Yes, we are related to her. She's my half-sister. Same dad, Donald Hugo Smith, different mother. Her dad and my mum married very young – when mum was just eighteen and dad nineteen. It didn't last and they divorced. My mum then married someone called Brierly, and James, who is no relation to Helen, different mum and dad, married her".

The inspector cut him short, he'd heard the distress in the man's voice. "Mr Smith, tell me where you live. I think it will be better for you if I come to your home. I'll bring a colleague with me to take notes. Do you have anyone with you?

"Yes, my daughter Janet".

"It'll take me an hour to reach you. I'll be as quick as I can and I have asked Sergeant Andy Boon to accompany you from the police station and stay with you until I get there".

Janet, as she was helping her dad out of the car said, "He sounds like a sensitive man. Strange, I thought all coppers could be bastards!"

As she left the police station Janet had called her husband Jack and he said he would join her at her father's home.

Janet had just settled her father down and gone to make a cup of tea for the policeman, and tea and a piece of toast for her father, when the doorbell rang. Upon opening it she saw a strange man, holding out his hand.

"Inspector Colin Jarvis. Is Sergeant Andy Boon here? Are you Janet?"

She nodded, "My dad's in the kitchen, come on through".

"Mr Smith, I understand you have mentioned a half-brother James, and your real brother. Tell me how they are involved with all of this".

"Bernard, he's the one who snatched the child, Hugo. Well we know now he 'snatched' him. At the time we didn't like it, but I knew he wouldn't harm his own nephew. James planned it all. I don't know what James has on Bernard but it must be pretty nasty for Bernard to agree to do this – that or the money James offered to share with him. James offered him £1 million. Offered me the same but I told him I wouldn't touch it with a barge pole!"

"After he 'snatched' him, what happened?

"He came here for the night. Told us, Janet and me, he was taking the kid to visit his dad. He said he would be leaving early to get across the channel".

May I ask, when you are so obviously against it all, why you didn't contact us before?"

"For one thing, I hadn't seen the press release. Janet told me about it, and for another, I didn't want to get involved, and I especially didn't want Janet and her family to get into trouble", said Keith as he pulled out a handkerchief.

"It's alright dad, just tell the inspector everything you know".

"Well Bernard left, taking the boy with him and I don't know what happened after that. I've tried calling him on his mobile and either he hasn't charged it or its broken and I can't get through".

"What about your other brother, James, have you spoken to him?"

"Yes, I think he's playing dumb. He says they aren't there, but I wouldn't believe a word that conniving vicious bastard says. If they aren't there, I don't know where the hell they are. Oh and one other strange thing, he said his brother-in-law was staying with him. Why do you think that is true?"

The inspector merely thanked him

"Sergeant Andy Boon will be staying on. If you can think of anything else, please tell him. I am not planning on arresting you Mr Smith, not at this stage anyway".

Chapter 14

hile the questioning of Mr Keith Smith went on, in France, James was having a foul day. He had been tense when Christiane began to nag him about another woman. "Where else had he been on Saturday and Sunday, not getting home until Monday morning, if he wasn't 'screwing' another woman? Why had he taken her car if not to confuse someone else's husband?" She went on and on, each accusation getting louder.

James began by being reasonable – he couldn't explain exactly, because it was a private matter.

"A private matter!" she screamed at him, "To do with your 'private parts' – without doubt! You are a liar and a cheat!"

"I'm not!" he shouted back. "I've been faithful to you!"

"You! Faithful! What about your poor wife? You used to come here with her and your children and pretend you go to the Bar, and you are with me! You don't know what *faithful* is!"

It had gone on and on. The neighbours would have heard everything. Not that it mattered, considering the other neighbours on the corner and those in the house behind them. The whole street had been witnesses to their arguments. Nobody would now turn a hair when he and Christiane fell out.

When she screamed at him again about her car, he retaliated by shouting, "Go and check the mileage, you stupid woman! I didn't go and visit a local woman, I went over to England! Well not all the way to England. I arranged to meet my brother. He was bringing my son Hugo to see me, but he didn't turn up".

"Well where is he? Where's your son?"

"I don't know, I tell you. I waited for several hours where we agreed to meet and he never came".

"I don't believe you. You are a liar and a cheat".

James knew she was right. He'd never planned to meet Bernard. Instead he had visited another woman. It had begun the week before at the Chaorce Golf Club. He'd been sitting at a table with a golfing friend and his non-playing wife, when the other man got up to go to the 'toilette', his wife said, as she passed a piece of paper with her mobile number on it,

"My husband is on a business trip to Italy for a few days next week – over next weekend. Why don't you come for dinner? I can offer you a bed".

James knew exactly which bed – hers. So he'd called her and gone. Later he was to regret it while trying to convince Christiane, and the English police he'd had nothing to do with the kidnapping, he realised it would be difficult to explain exactly where he had been.

The sound and the language got louder and hotter. The abuse became more and more lethal, until in the end, he'd blurted out he was trying to blackmail Helen into giving him three million euro's by kidnapping their son.

That silenced her. Christiane may not be a totally honest woman during her life, especially when it came to lovers – but even she was flabbergasted by his statement.

"You've kidnapped your own son – Hugo – three million euro's? You are disgusting! You are despicable! It is enough! I am leaving. I will *never* come back. I do not believe all English men are so bad – but *you – you are very bad!*"

"Please Christiane, don't go!" he pleaded.

She ignored him, and went upstairs to remove all her clothes and other things from the wardrobes and drawers. She came back down and completely ignored him, and phoned her brother.

"Phillipe, please come and collect all my things now. I am leaving James. Yes, he is a *'cochan'* – a pig! No, he didn't hit me, but he is horrible, terrible! Merci, a bientot! Au revoir."

Without another word, she proceeded to pile her belongings outside the house near the double front gates they locked every night. She ignored James's pleading. She simply turned her back on him and spat 'merde' at him when he approached her.

Her brother came and loaded up the trailer he was towing and without a single word, or look, Christiane loaded up her belongings, and followed him in her own car.

James knew the whole village would hear about their final row. He was afraid she would tell everyone about the kidnapping. Why, oh why had he been such a fool to blurt it out? Thank God they were in France – perhaps news of what he'd done wouldn't get back to England, he thought to himself.

Chapter 15

It was Tuesday morning and the house was eerily quiet. Rory was in France and keeping Alison up to date with what was going on. The inspector had been busy interviewing James's half-brother Keith. Helen and Jill, the sergeant, were sitting each clutching a mug of coffee.

"Helen, I am definitely guessing you believe your ex-husband is behind the kidnapping, it this right?"

Helen nodded, "Yes, I think I've known all along that he is capable of doing anything in order to get his own way".

"Do you feel like talking about it?", asked Jill.

"I think I would like to. I've kept so many things hidden, especially from my sister and her family. Daddy guessed about lots of things James was involved in, and thinking back, now that I know my father was married and divorced from James's mother, I think he was very sad about the way James was treating me and it may have shortened his life. He certainly was never the same after my mother died. James as you know is not related to me. He had a different father".

"Do you mind if I take some notes because some of the things you tell me, may be of use to the Guv?"

"No, I don't mind. I am prepared to 'dish the dirt' as they say".

"Right, begin when you are ready".

Helen took a sip of her coffee. "I am pretty sure James has been unfaithful ever since I met him. He finds it impossible to stick to one woman. I don't know whether it boosts his ego to seduce other women or he cannot help himself, but he just seems to have a desire to prove to himself he can get any woman he wants to. Looking back, I wonder if he really wanted to marry me, or he was looking over my shoulder at my father's wealth – probably the latter".

Helen paused while she stared out of the window. "I was very happy when I met James, the love of my life, I thought, and I believed he felt the same way about me, but looking back I think the only time he was really happy, was when he was in a casino. We went to Las Vegas several times and James always headed for the roulette table. I was content playing the fruit machines. Sometimes I would stand behind him watching the play, and honestly Jill I could almost feel the excitement going through him. I think that was the time he began visiting casinos in London. After that he was always asking for money, so I don't think he could have been very successful".

Helen glanced across at Jill who was listening and writing at the same time.

"Then there was the time when we went to a friend's house – at least I thought they were friends. Before we left home James made me change out of the slightly suggestive clothes I was wearing, saying my dress was too sexy. I thought at the time it was because he loved me so much he didn't want any of the guys looking at me. The dress he picked out for me was very dull and high necked. Anyway the party was fun and I was behaving myself, as he'd ordered me to do! No dancing and not too much to drink, then I realised I hadn't seen James for a while, so I went looking for him. He was in their dining room where the music was coming from. There were no lights on and it was very dark. I reached out and found the light switch and turned the wall lights on – and there was James with one of my girlfriends and it was obvious there had been more than dancing going on. Her off the shoulder dress was much lower than it should have been and James certainly had his hands where they shouldn't have been. Oh, Jill I couldn't believe it – it was horrible. James reacted first and shouted 'what the f…' and when he saw it was me he didn't back down – not then anyway, and say sorry".

Helen didn't notice that Jill's hands had clenched into a fist with her nails cutting into her hands.

"What did you do after this?"

"I think I switched the lights off and I fled. I grabbed my purse and ran home. We didn't live very far away. Then I locked myself in the bedroom and ignored his pleas for me to open the door. He kept saying that it was her fault and he'd had too much to drink – and so on. I buried my head under my pillow, but I couldn't sleep. Next day he said he was sorry and it would never happen again and I like a fool believed him".

"I think your coffee will be cold, would you like another?"

Helen shook her head. "It was much later, several years, I found out he'd used my money to buy a cottage to rent out. At the time I was pleased he was showing some interest in investing the money, that was until I found out he'd bought it in a village not far from us and installed his mistress in there!"

"Oh God, Helen what a dreadful, deceitful man!"

"That was only the beginning of it. For a while he behaved very well, taking me away on holidays to the Caribbean and the inevitable Vegas. I don't know if he met an Englishman in Vegas, but I think that was when he became very heavily involved with gambling. He joined a private members club in London and became much more secretive about where he was. By that time both Hugo and Amy had arrived and I was much too busy to care much. It was only when a couple of strange men arrived at our front door asking for him that I started to worry about what he was up to".

"Drugs?"

"No, I don't think so, but who knows, by that time James could have been involved with anything and I am pretty certain he was on cocaine which was causing mood swings. However, I think it was more to do with money James owed. He told me he needed half a million because he wanted to expand his business. My father had made me a partner in his writing projects and so I did have plenty of money – so I gave it to him. Around that time, my father took me out to lunch, just the two of us and I know he was hoping I'd open up and talk to him about James. But I couldn't Jill, I just couldn't! I know he would have helped me, but I didn't want him to know how bad James really was, so I kept it to myself, not even telling Alison. I now believe he knew much more than he was letting on".

Jill's phone rang and when she answered it Helen knew she was speaking to the Inspector.

"Hi Guv. I'm sitting talking to Helen now Sir. She's telling me a lot more about James's past life. Yes, I'll let her know you've called. Bye Sir".

"Then it got much worse. James came home one day and he was in a terrible state. Crying and almost incoherent and begging me to help him. He'd got in with a gambling cartel and he didn't know what to do. They had been accepting his debts because they knew he had a very wealthy wife, but they'd had enough and were now demanding their money back and had threatened to come after me and Hugo and Amy. They'd threatened him as well. I didn't ask him what they were planning for him, but it had to be nasty. I went into shock and just asked how soon they needed the money. James said next week. I felt numb. I didn't know who to turn to and I couldn't ask my father for help as he had been told he had terminal cancer and didn't have long to live. I didn't want to talk to Rory because he would have told me to say no. So I told James I would get him the money and that I would be seeing my solicitor and divorcing him. I'd had enough".

"I'm not surprised. So what did you do?"

"After James had left – he wanted to stay but I told him to go and visit his mistress. I didn't want him anywhere near the children or me. I packed the kids into the car and headed for my father's house. I felt safer there and I also hired a security firm to install a very sophisticated alarm system with cameras and lights everywhere on both houses. Next day I called my solicitor and told him to sort out the divorce papers. I said I would give James £1 million, which he's already had, and I'm not sure how much he's got left after paying off his friends, and would make over the cottage in France, which I haven't done yet, and would never do now. I think James thought it would be a great escape hole".

"So that's why he's in France now?" asked Jill.

"I guess so. I occasionally get a call from his French neighbour, Marie. She's a great gossiper and she hates James. My French isn't as good as James or Rory's and so I struggle a bit talking to her – she doesn't speak a word of English. I'm sure James has installed another woman in the cottage because it wouldn't be like him not to. I don't trust him Jill and the kidnapping and demand for £3 million has got to be him. What I don't know is who is helping him".

"By the way, the Guv said they were making some progress but still didn't know where Hugo and his kidnapper were, although they do now know his name and that he is a half-brother to James".

"That's weird. James has never mentioned anyone except his parents, both of whom are dead. Do you know Jill, I don't think he cares about us, well maybe Hugo, but I doubt it would bother him if something happened to me because before the final divorce goes through, which it will do very shortly, he would get my estate. He is scared for himself. He's always been a bully – and a coward".

Helen began to sob again and so Jill decided to wrap it up for the morning.

After the two women had some lunch, Helen suddenly said, "I've got something to show you. I haven't told anyone else about it but it may have some clues about James". She got up and unlocked a small cupboard in the corner of the room and pulled out what looked like a fairly thick folder and a notebook.

Jill was curious but waited for Helen to explain.

"Nobody has seen this since I found it after my father died. It is a portfolio of information about James and his activities. From the notebook I discovered a list of payments made to a private investigator. This was why I said earlier that my father must have known much more than he told me and he was just waiting for me to say something, which I didn't. I just didn't want my father to think badly of me and my choice in men".

"I am sure he would never have done that", replied Jill. "Does it give you a lot more information about your ex-husband?"

"Yes, masses. One thing which I didn't know was that James had gone bust and his business closed down. All of this happened a couple of years before dad died. So when James said he was off to work, he was lying. He was using any money I gave him to entertain other women, and I noticed that the rent from the cottage he bought, I now know for his mistress, was going into a separate account in his name. Oh Jill, what a gullible fool I have been!", she said as she opened up the notebook to show the policewoman.

"Helen, I think I need to call the guv and tell him about this. I'm sure he'll want to see it".

"Yes, you are right. It wasn't that I'd forgotten the paperwork, but didn't think it might be useful. I found out from the reports that James had given up his flat in London and was then living with his former secretary in her apartment".

Jill was busy dialling the inspector's number while Helen began going through the reports. The private investigator seemed to have done a good job, even including James's bank account details, making Helen wonder how he got all of the stuff.

"My guv is about to head on back here Helen. He thinks there must be something to catch our nasty kidnapping scoundrel!"

The two women began to methodically go through the papers. It was the parts about James's involvement with the men who had been bankrolling him that the reports became much nastier. They had been forcing James to do various illegal and disturbing things. They ranged from drug dealing – in big quantities, to money laundering and even recruiting underage girls to entertain much older men, many of whom had household names.

"I think James could well have done some blackmailing because he always seemed to have plenty of money", said Helen.

"Like he's doing to you?"

Helen just nodded.

"This is the bit that's most disturbing. Do you remember the stories about the man's body being pulled for the Thames? Somebody had broken all his fingers before he was dumped".

Jill said yes she did remember.

"Dad's chap somehow got to know that it was the same people who did it, were part of the organised crime group that James got himself involved with. No wonder he was scared to death of what they might do to him".

"Why did they allow James to move to France?"

"That's in here too. I think James might have been becoming a nuisance and it suited the bosses to let him 'retire' and live in France. I felt better that he was out of the way of the children and I. There are numerous names and contact details in these notes as well".

"Whew Helen, a lot of this stuff may have nothing to do with our case, but I bet there will be other branches in the police force who will have a field day!"

"I did try and talk to dad's PI after dad died, but he said he couldn't talk to me as he had been employed by my father and as far as he was concerned, he'd fulfilled his brief and closed the case. There is another thing – a letter from my father to me. It was at the bottom of the papers underneath everything else. Would you like to see it?"

"If you would like me to. If it's not too personal".

"Here. You read it. I'm just going out into the garden for a little while"

As Helen left the room, Jill carefully removed the letter from its envelope and began to read –

Darling Helen, it is hard to know where to start except to say that I have been very sad watching your relationship with James get worse. I have to say I never liked him from day one, but you seemed to be so much in love I didn't want to spoil it. After my first disastrous marriage, I was very young and like you thought I had met the love of my life, I only wanted the very best for you. You have always been my favourite – I think you knew this, and you were seven years older than I was when I was forced into marrying?, She was pregnant you see. Big mistake on my part. Anyway, we muddled along and had two sons, Bernard and Keith. She was a tyrant though, constantly nagging and demanding that I get a job earning more money, until one day I snapped, packed a bag and left. I was never good enough for her. Please don't think badly of me, I continued to support them until Keith was eighteen but never went back.

I met your mother a year or so later, and she was everything I'd dreamed of. Kind and caring and encouraging.

Getting back to James, although I hate writing about him, I had no idea of the connection. I knew him as James Brierly. I'd never bothered to find out my ex-wife's new married name, which was Brierly. It turned out he was as evil as his mother, and I have wondered many times if she deliberately pushed him towards you. I will never know, she died many years ago.

When I discovered the link, I watched him very closely hoping he genuinely loved you, but I am sad to say, I don't think he ever did. Like his mother it was all about money – money and James first!

I wanted to understand who you had married and so got myself a private investigator who turned up a great many things I did not want to know about the 'filthy bastard'. The women, gambling, the lies and deceit he practised everywhere he went.

I always hoped you would be able to open up and talk to me, but you didn't or couldn't and I respect you for that. You are my daughter and we both suffer from pride. I could have no more talked to my parents and admitted my early mistakes, than you could tell me.

Anyway, my darling daughter, I am leaving all the research about James in the hopes these documents will open your eyes and you and my beautiful grandchildren enjoy great lives without him. And for you, my dying wish is that you do meet someone you can love and respect.

With love, Daddy

Jill, with tears in her eyes, pushed the letter back into the envelope, before going out into the garden to find Helen and to tell her the inspector had arrived.

Helen indicated she would prefer to stay outside, and so Jill rejoined the inspector where the two of them began to go through the paperwork and Helen's father's letter. In the end they decided to take everything back to HQ, except for the letter which they left on the desk.

Helen seemed to have gone back into her shell. For a while she remained in the garden, sitting on the seat where Hugo had last been seen by Alison.

Chapter 16

fter Christiane had stormed off, James checked his mailbox, more bills – and, a nasty solicitor's letter from England. Hall, Roche and Bates, Solicitors, of Salisbury, were threatening to take action against him on behalf of a former lover whose child he knew to be his.

Yes, Jodi had come back into his life. She had been the cause of the end of his riotous living in London. He thought back to that Friday night when Helen had come up to London and overheard him talking to Jodi. Of course, he'd promised never to see Jodi again. He'd said that he would mend his ways and never be unfaithful again. Helen had been satisfied with all his declarations of love – while *he* had never been satisfied with just one woman! He hadn't even been faithful to his lovers! He'd always gone running between Helen and at least one or two others.

Jodi, who had been genuinely in love with him, had been prepared to wait for about six months before he'd been able to meet up with her again. By this time Helen was six months pregnant. She hadn't been well at first, feeling sick for about the first three months. Her parents became quite worried, and when her father was invited to a 'book signing' in Florida, they had persuaded her to go with them for a week in the sunshine. James had been invited as well, but he cried off with the excuse that he had a big presentation to prepare for a large company.

Helen had some doubts about leaving James by himself. But he expressed his undying love for her and told her how very busy he would be, working long hours to get the presentation together.

James had driven Helen and her parents to Heathrow and seen them off to the U.S. Then, by prior arrangement, he dashed to a discreet little French restaurant, to meet up with Jodi.

Of course, as he had planned, they drifted from the restaurant, to her flat. Jodi had decided beforehand that she wouldn't allow James straight back into her bed. He needed to be taught a lesson – to feel some of the hurt she'd experienced when he cleared off from London, leaving her for his wife. However, after a couple of bottles of excellent red wine between them, it seemed natural, when James said he couldn't drive after drinking so much, that they had taken a taxi back to her flat – inevitably, they had ended up in her bed.

Jodi was a good lover, wild and inventive and James fell into her arms with a passion he'd forgotten he had. Perhaps it was the combination of the wine, and the lack of sex he'd been having with Helen, that he responded to her touch with excitement and pleasure way beyond his dreams.

He stayed with Jodi until the next morning – each enjoying the renewal of their lovemaking, James then knew he couldn't stay away from her. As he drove back to Salisbury, he began to make his plans. He knew Helen wouldn't countenance his travelling to London often, and so, if he couldn't go to London, then he had to persuade Jodi to come to Wiltshire. He would go and see her again while Helen was away with her parents, and try and persuade her to move. He would look around for a cottage to buy, and then tell Helen he'd decided to go into buying a property to let out. She had already said they ought to be investing in something. Jodi could move in and he would visit her there. Helen had never seen Jodi and so she wouldn't recognise her; and besides, if she ever saw the tenancy agreement, she wouldn't realise it was James's former lover living in the cottage because Jodi's real name was Jane Anne Dowd.

That afternoon, back in Wiltshire, James began to tour the local Estate Agents, looking for a suitable property. He decided he didn't want a cottage in a village too close to where he and Helen lived – just in case he was seen and recognised by any of their acquaintances when visiting Jodi after she'd moved in. Of course he could always say she'd got a problem with her gas fire or some such thing – but he felt that a bit further away would be better.

He chose details of three or four cottages he thought might tempt Jodi and, on the following day after work, he made his way up to London. James didn't believe he'd be caught out because he had already phoned Helen in Florida and knew she and her parents had a full day doing 'book signings' followed by a dinner where they were the celebrity guests. Before ringing off he professed his great love for Helen, told her he was missing her dreadfully and couldn't wait to hold her in his arms again. He then enquired about the baby – was she still feeling OK? Just a bit tired? Well, he'd talk to her again the next day. He then put the phone down and with a smirk on his face, he got into his car to head for London and completely forgot about Helen, so absorbed was he with his plans for a love nest with Jodi.

Jodi had been adamant she wouldn't move from London. She had a great job, which she loved. No, she wasn't going to be persuaded. James, who, not for nothing was known as a charmer, plied her with wine over a beautiful dinner in a very expensive restaurant overlooking the river. Later, back at her flat again, he made passionate love to her and told her he couldn't live without her. He even went as far as saying that when he got his business on a firmer basis, he would leave Helen for her.

Jodi relented a little. All right, she'd just come down and look at some of the cottages with him. Yes, she would go back with him the next morning and they could go house hunting. James, lying beside her in bed, clenched his fist under the sheet and mentally shouted, yes! He knew he'd won.

Jodi had chosen a cottage just outside the village of East Knoyle in Wiltshire – some twenty miles from where James and Helen lived. The cottage was delightful, with a pretty garden was surrounded by a high brick wall. It was reached by a narrow lane and not overlooked by any other houses. The cottage, about two hundred years old, had low beams and a large inglenook fireplace in the sitting room. But, the room they both fell in love with was the bedroom, where the ceiling had been raised to follow the roof line and the old cross beam in the centre was exposed and hung a good eight feet below the angled plaster that formed the new ceiling.

The price was good and James made an offer that was accepted. Solicitor's names exchanged, and the sale and purchase were underway before Helen had even left the United States for home.

James knew he had to be a little careful about letting the cottage to Jodi. It. wouldn't do to be seen to have already got her in tow when he'd originally purchased the place. He needed to go through a Letting Agent, with Jodi enquiring before anyone else did. Again, James congratulated himself – his plans ran smoothly and Jodi duly moved in.

Helen had been delighted with James's plan for buying a cottage and letting it out. James was also delighted – he now had two women available for his needs!

Hugo was born a few months later and Helen became preoccupied with her new baby. James had more freedom, and a pretty secretary ready and available was added to his list of conquests. James smiled to himself when he thought of Emily Jones, a gorgeous little red head, as fiery as her hair. Helen never found out about her, but her rotten father suspected an affair and forced the situation by finding Ms Jones a better paid job elsewhere.

Jodi had managed to get herself an excellent position as personal assistant to the Managing Director of a new house builder. The firm was expanding rapidly, building 'up market' exclusive developments around Salisbury and Winchester mainly. She'd even got involved in the furnishing and decorating of the Show Houses. She loved her job, but as the years went by, she began to think more about herself as a woman and the fact that her 'biological clock' was ticking away. She broached the subject of James leaving Helen, on several occasions, but he'd always got plenty of excuses! Jodi decided to take fate into her own hands – she deliberately stopped taking the pill. She knew Helen was pregnant again and jealousy and envy took over. If Helen could have James's baby – so could she!

Of course, she didn't tell James she was trying to trap him into marriage.

James was livid when she broke the news to him that she was also pregnant. They nearly had a complete falling out and it was only the threat made by Jodi that she would go to Helen with the news of their ongoing affair, which stopped James in his tracks. He was still angry, but decided to conceal it. He made plenty of excuses. Said how worried he was about her. Called her 'darling', but did not, as she had hoped, mention anything about leaving Helen for her. James wasn't stupid. He had the privilege he'd craved, business was going well and, with two women pregnant, he'd have time to chat up the local MP's wife who had thrown out lures to him!

Wow, he thought as he let the memories roll. He'd had one hell of a life and got away with so much. Part of the excitement he felt was the double, or even treble, life he lived. He'd also continued with his gambling. Now only through a local bookie, who most months, was delighted to have him as a client. Some months James was up, but most months down. While he'd stayed with Helen, and her 'bloody' father, he'd kept his gambling under control!

James carried a beer and his lunch of pate, cheese and a baguette out on to the patio outside his French house while he continued to reminisce.

He'd insisted on having a blood test on himself and Jodi's baby. After all, *he* wasn't prepared to pay for somebody else's child! It *was* his, of course, and so in order to keep Jodi quiet – he'd paid out – until he'd moved to France! This was why he'd received the official letter this morning.

Helen had eventually found out about Jodi and her baby. It was about the time of her father's death and led to her finally kicking James out of her life. She'd only heard of his affair by accident when somebody at a party mentioned 'Jodi'. Helen stiffened at the name. The speaker went on to say what a charming woman she was. Helen enquired about husband and family. "No, she hasn't a husband although she does have a small child." Helen casually asked where she lived and the same kind informant replied, "In a small cottage near Shaftesbury, just outside East Knoyle, I believe."

Helen felt anger and rage flow through her. She quickly excused herself from the party and went home. James followed shortly after. By the time he got there, Helen already had suitcases out and was throwing his clothes into them. James knew why. He'd seen Helen react to something said at the party and, after she left, he'd wandered over to talk to Gillian, the woman Helen had been talking to. Gillian realised she'd said something to upset Helen and quite openly told James the gist of their conversation.

James fumed at the woman, "Why the hell couldn't you keep your bloody mouth shut?" And as he drove home he raged at 'stupid women' and life in general – but not for one moment did he blame himself.

James did not bother to argue with Helen. He simply took his bags and drove over to Jodi's, who greeted him happily.

James basked in her pleasure, but, James being James, got bored with that and before too long, he'd made his excuses and gone up to town for a couple of nights. This was where he made his biggest mistake – he got back in touch with his gambling friends. They were delighted to see him and were equally happy to take his money off him!

All this had happened a couple of years before. James fled to France to escape from Jodi and his gambling debts. It was these problems that had led to his plan to get even more money from Helen. She couldn't believe he'd already gone through the one million pounds she'd given him when their separation became legal and had refused to give him any more, so he had decided to kidnap Hugo. This plan should come to fruition in three days from now! He'd be able to pay of his debts to his 'friends' in London, sort out Jodi and, be in funds again.

James thought about his plans as he pottered around his garden all afternoon, avoiding the glares of various neighbours, who passed by on the road outside his house. About 9am on Tuesday morning, he decided to phone his brothers. He tried Keith's number first, but only got the answering service asking him to leave a message, which he did – just requesting Keith to phone him in France when he returned.

Bernard was next on the list, but as before, the message he got was that the phone was probably turned off.

"Where the hell are they?" James said, out loud. What he didn't know was that Keith had already talked to the police and the net was closing in on James – from more directions than he realised!

Chapter 17

Dinner eaten and washed up, James was about to go and lock the gate and close his shutters, when his front door banged open. Startled he looked up, expecting it to be Christiane – or worse one of her brothers. It was neither. Two totally strange men – 'thugs' barged into his house, one of them shutting the door behind them.

James thinking they were locals, spoke to them in French. The men answered in English.

"Where", they demanded, "was the money promised to 'his friends' in London – those kind men who had 'generously' underwritten his gambling debts".

James was speechless. How the hell had they found him? In France it wasn't just the case of looking up the name in the telephone directory, you had to know the name of the village.

Before he could ask, they answered his unspoken question.

"We called your girlfriend, the one you dumped. She happily gave us this address".

James had been thinking earlier on the day, that things couldn't get any worse – but they had!

The thugs walked threateningly towards James. He was terrified as he backed away , unable to go any further when his back hit the wall. He was a lying, cheating, unfaithful man and a complete coward.

"I'm getting the money on Friday afternoon," he blurted out. "They'll have it as soon as it is in my bank account".

"And how do you expect 'our friends' will believe that?"

"They must! I promise. I won't let them down! They'll get every penny back!", he cried out as he tried to retreat further away from them.

"I think we had better show him how upset 'our friends' are, don't you?" , asked Joe, the bigger of the two.

"Yes", replied Tony. "I think '*our friends*' would want us to make sure he understands very clearly what his obligations are".

James began to plead with them. "Please, please don't hurt me! I promise they'll get the money – all of it…." He had to stop there because Joe hit him hard in the stomach. James went down coughing and choking. He doubled up, holding his stomach. Tony put his foot in his groin.

"That was from Danny," said Joe as he kicked James hard in the face.

James screamed out, his head exploded with pain. His dinner and the wine he'd drunk, vomited out of his mouth. Another kick came in and broke his nose and, blessedly for him, he passed out.

How long he lay there, he didn't know, but when he came to, he thought he heard the church clock strike eleven.

James crawled through his own vomit and blood, which had poured from his face and nose. He dragged himself up on to a chair and sat there in agonising pain. He wondered if he'd ever be able to make love to a woman again – the pain was so strong from that area of his body.

Eventually, he managed to drag himself to the downstairs bathroom. By holding on to the washbasin with both hands shaking, he raised his head to inspect the damage to his face. He was appalled. His nose was swollen beyond recognition. The surrounding flesh was rapidly turning black and blue. He had a deep cut under one eye, which began bleeding again as he stood up. Taking one hand unsteadily off the edge of the basin, he ran warm water into it and began gently to clean up the bleeding mess left by the two thugs, who mercifully appeared to have gone.

Having cleaned up his face, he turned to the rest of his body. With fear in his mind, he stripped off his filthy clothes. His stomach and genitals were bruised and battered, but as far as he could see, there had been no bleeding. He couldn't tell what damage they might have done internally.

James reached for his dressing gown hanging on the back of the bathroom door. Staggering back into his kitchen, he picked up a glass; half filled it with Scotch and swigged down several pain killers. He choked as the whisky hit his stomach, but kept the fiery liquid down. Refilling the glass he sipped more slowly and then practically crawled his way through to the bed so recently occupied by his brother-in-law, Rory.

"God, it seems so long ago that he was here", muttered James. He remembered that he'd meant to phone Keith again during the evening. It was too late now, and besides, he didn't think he could get off the bed again to get the phone. Thank goodness he'd brought the whisky bottle with him. Pouring himself another large drink, he lay on the bed in far too much pain to drop off to sleep yet – that would come when the combination of the pills and the alcohol took effect.

His last thought, as he fell asleep was – what a complete fool I've been. Jodi demanding money and his gambling acquaintances really on his back – and then having to kidnap his own son in order to force Helen to pay up. And where the 'bloody hell' *was* his son? He didn't think Bernard was dangerous, but it was very worrying he'd cleared off with Hugo and nobody seemed to know where he'd gone to.

Chapter 18

Janet, and her husband Jack, were both very relieved to be allowed to remain at her father's home. Janet and her father Keith had been questioned for hours and both were exhausted. She felt so ashamed of not having returned Hugo to his mother on the night of the kidnap.

"James had been so plausible in his lies," she'd explained, "I hadn't really understood anything, until it was too late – Hugo had already been taken away by Uncle Bernard."

She had willingly handed over her passport, which Jack had the forethought to bring, and had promised to remain at home until the case was resolved. Jack had also given a written undertaking to make sure her word was kept.

Jack helped her into the car at about 11.30pm to head home. He had held her in his arms before opening the passenger door. She felt so lucky to have a husband like him. Poor, poor Helen to have married a bastard like James, if – *when* - this is all over, she can forgive me, I'd like to get to know her and I would certainly like to see Hugo again, these were her last thoughts before falling into an exhausted sleep.

Keith too, was relieved to be allowed to stay in his home, all be it with a policeman to keep an eye on him, when he could have been sitting in a locked cell right now. He had told them everything he could, not to save his own skin, because he thought he probably deserved it if they did send him to prison. In fact, he'd tried to do everything possible to find the child and return him to his mother.

During the late evening he and the police had discussed ways of getting James back to England. They knew it was unlikely he'd come of his own free will, but they had to trick him somehow. There wasn't time to go to the French authorities because they only had two and a bit days before the kidnap deadline, and besides they wanted to arrest the man on English soil. At around midnight, the inspector called for his police driver and headed back, first to his office, and then to try and get a few hours' sleep.

What had been devised was for Keith to phone James and try to frighten him to return. Keith knew James loved Hugo very much and perhaps, if Keith could get across the message that Hugo was in real danger, James might, just might, be tempted to dash back to England.

With this in mind, the police decided it would be better for Keith to telephone him from home – just in case James decided to call him back. So, on Thursday morning at just after 8.30 am in England – 9.30 am in France – Keith picked up the phone and called James. It was funny, he thought, James was both his half-brother *and* his brother-in-law. Keith *hated* him though, whatever the relationship. Remembering all the times he'd baled James out financially, he knew how fraudulent and deceitful he was. Even beginning to think that, once James got hold of the money, neither Bernard nor he would actually see any of it. Not that he would touch it!

The phone rang and rang. Keith began to think James had gone out, however, he let it go on ringing. Just as he was about to hang up, the phone was answered. Keith was relieved it was James and not his 'fancy woman'.

James answered. At first Keith didn't realise who it was, the voice sounded so odd. Of course, being at the other end of the phone he couldn't see the state of James's face!

James had been in the process of trying to clear up the mess made by his own vomit and blood. It had taken several minutes just to get a bucket and cloth and to actually kneel down on the floor to wash off the disgusting mess. The pain in his groin had made him cry out when he'd stood in front of the lavatory earlier on. He began to sob again as he bent over to wash the floor. When the phone went, he'd decided to let it ring, but it went on and on and so eventually, he'd struggled to stand up, holding first on to a chair and then on to the table. He made his way painfully to the phone and through a swollen mouth, with at least one broken tooth, he'd answered in the French manner, "Allo?"

Keith, with the constable beside him, said, "James? Is that you James?"

"Yes," Came the muffled answer.

"You don't sound very much like James!" responded Keith.

"Had a fall. Hit my head."

"Oh, I'm sorry to hear that, but I've some bad news for you. I've heard from Bernard. You've *got* to come home! It's about the boy."

James struggled to ask, "What about the boy?"

"Bernard says he's had enough. He says he's getting scared. He just wants to get rid of the boy and leave the country."

"What do you mean, get rid of the boy?" slurred James.

"Get rid – kill – murder him! Bury the body and scarper!"

"No! He can't do that!"

"Well he says he can. He says he's worried you'll keep all the money anyway. I've begged him to wait. He says he will, but only if you come and join him – so as you can go together! He says if you are with him, he can make sure he'll get his share."

"Where is he?"

Again Keith found it hard to understand his half-brother.

"That must have been a pretty bad fall you had. I can hardly tell what you're saying."

"Where is he?" repeated James, slowly.

"I don't know. When I asked him that, he just said – 'You've got eight and a half hours to get James to your house. If he's not there by the time I phone at 8pm tonight, I'll just dispose of the boy and be on my way.' Then he rang off and I didn't have a chance to ask anything else."

Keith heard a groan from James. "What's that?"

"Nothing. Just sitting down."

"Look James! I *really* believe him! You've got to come over! He's your son, after all. He's a nice little chap – but he's *not mine – he's yours!*"

"OK. OK!"

"Are you coming?"

"Don't know. Yes. Yes, I'll *have* to come, won't I!"

"Right. Right! Good. Come here. Look, shall I book a ferry for you?"

"No, I'll come by the tunnel – quicker."

"OK. Get here as soon as you can, I'll be waiting. Look, give me your mobile number so I can contact you on the way if I need to."

James mumbled his number and Keith had to ask a couple of times to repeat some of the numbers. He repeated it back to James who finally said, "Yes," and with that Keith hung up and turned to the copper.

"He's coming. You heard? I'm not sure when, but he said he'll come."

"Well done Sir. You were very convincing. Now, perhaps, while I call the inspector, would you make us both a cup of tea?"

Constable Boon picked up the phone and dialled his senior officer.

"He's made the call Guv….." "Yes, it went very well indeed…." "Yes, Mr Brierly has agreed to come back – by the tunnel he said…." "No, Mr Smith couldn't get an exact time. He did get his mobile number though – said he would call him if he heard anything else…." "Yes, we thought he could phone him on his mobile in an hour or so, just to find out how he's progressing.".…. "Yes, OK Guv. I'll stay here with him. I think he's exhausted. We're going to have a cup of tea and then I'll offer to make us some breakfast and after that persuade him to go to bed."

"And what will you do, Boon?"

"Oh, I'll have a look at his newspaper, watch a little TV and wait for the phone to ring," replied the constable, with aplomb.

"Right you are then, but don't you answer the phone. Contact me if anything happens." Inspector Jarvis hung up the phone, still smiling to himself. He was a good copper – Constable Boon, which was why the Inspector had picked him out to go with Helen's half-brother. He'd fix breakfast all right, *and* he would get any other information he could by just chatting to Keith Smith. In the informal atmosphere of his home, Mr Smith might well remember things he hadn't thought about under the pressure of formal questioning by the inspector.

It was good to get James's mobile phone number. They, or rather Keith, would get in touch with him 'en route' from France. In that way they would have a better idea of when he might be crossing and so have customs ready to pick him up. They'd let Mr Smith have two or three hours rest and then get him on the phone again to Mr James 'bloody' Brierly!

The inspector needed to make a couple of phone calls. One to Helen to find out what make, colour and model car James had and, if possible, the number. He would then phone Rory. He might know if James ever drove a French car. He was cunning enough to come over in something other than his own vehicle.

"Please Jill can you ask Helen if she can you give me any details about James's car?" Inspector Jarvis asked.

When asked by Jill, Helen replied quietly. "He's got a black BMW and his number is J4MES.

Jill handed the phone over to Helen, "It's the gov".

"Do you know if he ever drove any other cars in France?"

"I think he sometimes drove his girlfriend's car, but I don't know what she's got. I'm sorry."

"Don't worry. I was going to telephone Rory. He is over there and might have seen her car. Oh, by the way, Mr Keith Smith has persuaded him to come back to the UK. This is why I'm anxious to find out what he might be driving. We'll let him get over here and then arrest him."

"Oh please let him find Hugo for me

"Bye Helen. I'll talk to you later."

Inspector Jarvis called Rory, who was still in Chablis. He had several wine purchases to collect later, he said.

Upon enquiring about cars, Rory replied, "I expect you know about James's black BMW with its personalised number plates?"

"Yes. Helen told me. I just wondered whether he might be cunning enough to come over in something else."

"Well, he might I suppose. His French girlfriend has a bright 'turquoise/blue coloured Peugeot."

"I don't suppose you've any idea of the number, do you, Mr Johnson?"

"No, except that it is bound to have '89' on the plate. That would indicate it comes from North Burgundy – the Chablis area."

"Thanks for that information, we'll know what to look out for then."

"So, he's coming back?"

"Yes. We got Mr Keith Smith to telephone him and persuade him to come over. I can count on your discretion not to let on, can't I, Sir?"

"Of course, I hate the bastard! I think I'd better head to Maligny right now so that I am ready to follow him".

"Right, Rory. I'll need to get on and talk to our associates in Dover. Good bye and thanks."

Inspector Jarvis picked up the phone again and asked for the Superintendent of the Kent Division. Fifteen minutes later, he was satisfied that a discreet plan was in place to catch Mr James Brierly as soon as he arrived back in the UK. They would be watching both the tunnel crossing and the ferry ports as well – just in case he changed his mind about how he crossed the Channel.

Chapter 19

James put down the phone after speaking to his brother Keith. He was angry. Angry with the pain he was feeling. Furious with Keith for putting pressure on him and angry with Helen for not sharing her wealth and particularly angry with Bernard. How dare he go off with Hugo? That wasn't part of the plan at all! And the fact that he brought Janet and her children into the mess was completely wrong! He felt he could personally kill Bernard right now – brother, or no brother!

He was angry with his whole family, especially his mother. He blamed her for everything. She had been a strong domineering woman and he suspected it was because of the nagging and demanding she'd made on his stepfather that had pushed him away. Then she's married his father, Albert Brierly and he fared no better. James believed it was she who'd made him into the uncaring man he turned out to be. Her fault that he thought the world owed him everything. Nothing was good enough for James, never satisfied with anything, not even marrying Helen – oh no, he had taken risks because this was the only way he got any excitement.

He despised both his half-brothers because he knew they wouldn't stand up to him. He'd got as much money as he could from Helen and her father and then went further by getting heavily involved with gambling. This again he blamed on everyone else – if they'd been reasonable about money he wouldn't be in the mess he was.

He knew what he was going to do. He would go back to England and he would go along with Bernard – so far, anyway. Somehow he would get rid of Bernard. James was totally ruthless. Bernard was right. James had never had any intention of sharing the £3 million with his brothers. He'd planned all along to put the money into a bank account 'in his name' and then disappear. Leave England; leave France – and vanish. He'd planned to take Christiane with him, but now she'd gone, perhaps after all it was for the best anyway. There were plenty of other women he could find – they were always sending out signals to him!

As far as the money was concerned, he needed it all. He owed over half a million in gambling debts, which was why those thugs had beaten him up.

Painfully he finished clearing up the blood and vomit from the kitchen floor. He staggered up the stairs to his wardrobe to collect various things. Passport, bank books, and the number of the bank account he had opened ready to receive the £3 million along with various other things he valued. He didn't expect he would ever return to the house in France. Oh no – South America was beckoning him! Helen could have the house. It was only worth about £50,000 – 'chicken feed' to what he was taking off her!

He decided to drop a note through his next door neighbour's letterbox to ask her to clear out his fridge and cupboards and take what she wanted.

The letter written, he pushed a 100 euro currency note in with it and dropped it in her letterbox, along with his house keys.

All this took a little while and it was about 10.45 am before he drove away in his black BMW with the distinctive plates. Rory had been sitting waiting in a turn off to one of the vineyards when he saw James passing the end of the track.

As James headed north along back roads towards Tonnerre, he was relieved his car was automatic with cruise control – much easier to drive.

He passed through a couple of villages and then along the road that ran parallel with the TGV rail track for some miles. He watched with satisfaction as two of their amazing looking trains went by in opposite directions. He'd miss seeing them he thought. It was always fun to see them go by so close to the road.

Through Tonnerre, he cut across to Chaorce, passing near the golf club he'd patronised for quite a few years. He thought about the set of golf clubs he'd left behind in the garage at Maligny. He felt a little remorse in abandoning them, but he knew they would only be an encumbrance. Anyway, he thought selfishly, with the money I get from Helen, I can purchase myself the best set money can buy! His mind wandered with the anticipation and pleasure of choosing between Calloway's or Taylor Made's or perhaps Pings or other expensive makes of clubs.

He reached the autoroute near Troyes, wincing in severe pain when he lent out to take a ticket to pay for using the toll road.

"Damn those bastards!" he cried out to himself. "Danny shouldn't have set those 'effing' pigs on to me – he knew I'd find the money to pay him without that!" Actually James had never had any real intention of paying his debts. He'd got enough money to fly from Europe to South America and then he'd draw on the £3 million in the bank account.

James pulled into a rest area just north of Reims. There are so many rest areas on the Autoroutes that they are very rarely busy, and James was pleased to find this one deserted, although an HGV pulled in after him, followed by Rory. James didn't notice him as he staggered out of his car and headed towards the generally revolting 'hole in the floor' type lavatories the rest areas are blessed with.

Having relieved himself, although he wouldn't have called it relief, because the pain was still appalling, he shuffled back to his car. He was in a hurry, but he knew he had to take something to relieve his pain and was glad he'd thought to put a bottle of Evian in the car, which he used to wash down several more painkillers. While taking another swig of the bottled water, his mobile phone went off. Choking and panicking he blurted out. "Who the hell is phoning me?" James had forgotten he'd given Keith his number.

Switching it on, he said, "Allo?"

"Hallo James. Is that you?" asked his brother.

"Yes. What do you want? Has something happened to Hugo?"

"No. No – at least, not yet", replied Keith increasing the pressure.

"What do you mean – not yet? Have you heard from Bernard again?"

"Yes," said Keith, lying to him. "Where are you? Are you on your way?"

"Yes, I'm just north of Reims. I'd just stopped in a rest area to take some painkillers."

"Painkillers? What the hell are you taking *them* for?"

"Had an accident – car."

"What? Not your BMW?"

"No, another one – my BMW's OK. Why are we talking about cars? Bernard – what did he say?"

"He only called to ask if you were on your way. I told him yes. He wants to know what time you are likely to be here so he can talk to you."

"Why can't he phone me on my mobile like you're doing?"

"Not a good signal," answered Keith. "Anyway, what time do you think you'll arrive?"

"Don't know. I might have to wait for a place on the train. Tell Bernard I'm on my way as quickly as I can get there."

"OK, OK. Look, will you phone me when you know the channel crossing time, just in case Bernard phones again before you get here."

"Why can't you contact him and tell him I'm definitely on my way?"

"He wouldn't give me his number. I just have to rely on him calling me. Just get here. OK? From the way Bernard was ranting on, I'm really scared about what he might do to the kid."

"Keith, please, *please*, ask him to wait. I'm coming – just tell him that!"

Keith had already hung up.

He turned to the policeman at his side. You'd better call your boss. He's definitely using the channel tunnel. I've asked him to call me when he knows the departure time.

The Constable picked up the phone to speak to Inspector Jarvis to let him know the latest developments.

"He says he just north of *'Reems'*, guv. He'd stopped at a rest area north of the city. Said something about a car accident and taking painkillers.".….. "Yes, Mr Smith was a bit puzzled about that".….. "No, it wasn't in his BMW – I understand he's driving that now." He heard the inspector heave a sigh of relief.

"Thank goodness for that. We'd have had more of a problem if he'd been driving something else," remarked the inspector.

The constable muttered something derogatory.

"OK, Boon – that's enough!"

"Sorry, guv. Anyway, his brother has asked him to phone as soon as he knows what time the train is leaving."

"Fine, and just for your information Andy, we've sent some plainclothes officers over to France on both ferry companies and to the Tunnel, to watch out for him."

"Thanks, Boss," chuckled the constable. He knew he was back in the inspector's good books when he'd called him by his Christian name – Andy. "We'll let you know immediately we've spoken to him again. I guess it'll probably be in two to three hours' time. Bye, guv."

"Bye, Andy."

Right, thought the inspector as he picked up the phone to call his contact in Dover. It's an hour later in France, so we must bear that in mind. As far as he could remember from trips he'd made to France, the train only took about a half an hour to cross. But then there would be the loading and unloading times as well.

After speaking to his colleague, Inspector Jarvis thoughtfully picked up the phone to contact Rory.

"Hello Rory, is all good with you?"

"Yes, he's a few cars ahead of me. I'm following but not too close".

"Just curious, Mr Johnson. When you saw Mr Brierly, did he say anything about a car accident?"

"No. Absolutely not. I am fairly sure the two thugs who beat him will have done some severe damage to him. In fact, I am surprised he is able to drive at all. From what his neighbour saw, he was in bad shape. Why?"

"Well, it appears that he's taking painkillers to control pain after a 'car accident'. At least that was what he told Keith.

"He certainly wasn't in any pain when I last saw him – except, perhaps, a hangover on Monday morning, but nothing else."

"Well, it's only Thursday morning now, so whatever's happened, has taken place during the last forty-eight hours. Odd, isn't it?"

"Look, inspector, would you like me to phone his house in France just in case his French girlfriend is there, and try and get an update".

"If you wouldn't mind, Sir. But please be careful what you say."

"I'll call you right back, inspector. Good bye."

About ten minutes later, Rory phoned the inspector back.

"The whole thing stinks", he said. "When I phoned, expecting to talk to Christiane, I was surprised to hear Marie, the lady from next door, answer the phone. She's a great gossip and told me the lot. Apparently, James and Christiane had a big row on Tuesday and Christiane's brother came round to collect her and her things and she's cleared off. I understand that the insults thrown by both sides could be heard by the whole village - let alone the street! We had quite a few 'ooh la, la's' while Marie described neighbours opening their shutters and windows to listen in. Christiane has told everyone that he's a liar and a cheat."

The inspector interrupted with, "Serves him right."

Rory continued. "Then later on yesterday evening, when Marie was just closing her shutters, she saw two big men stop outside James's house. The car had English number plates, she said. She called out to her husband, Louis, and asked him if he knew who the men were. He said he didn't know. Marie said she rushed upstairs to look out of the window to see better. The men just walked into James's courtyard outside his house. They didn't knock at the door – just walked straight in. She and Jacques heard some shouting and furniture being knocked around, and then, after a few minutes, the two men came out, got into their car and drove away. She said, that she'd asked her husband, if they should go and see if James was OK, but he'd said no – whatever had happened to him, served him right. He'd never, ever, Louis said, with a shrug of his shoulders, liked James for the way he'd treated his wife, Helen. Marie agreed with her husband and they later went to bed. She said she'd planned to go round this morning to see James after she got back from visiting the doctor, but by that time he'd gone. Not only gone, but he'd left her a note saying to take what she wanted from the house, because he'd never be back!"

"Wow!" said the inspector. "Two men – who do *you* think they were?"

"Someone from James's past, I imagine. Someone he's deliberately cheated. Anyway, one other thing – when I asked about whether he had a car accident, she said 'No – it was probably the two men'. She also told me that the neighbour who lived opposite him had been watching from behind her lace curtains this morning and had seen him walking very slowly as though he was in a lot of pain. And – you should have seen his face – it was terrible! Sounds as though someone else got to James before I did!"

"Now, now Rory, let someone else deal with him. We don't want you being done for assault! But thanks for your help. It looks as though we'll be watching out for a black BMW with a driver sporting a battered face! Good bye again – and enjoy the drive through France. Let me know when you are turning off the A26 and on to the A16 and approaching the channel tunnel terminus"

"I was thinking about that. What if there is a long queue waiting to board?"

"We've thought about that. We are planning to funnel him into the lane reserved for special passengers, a sort of upgrade to business class if you like. You must follow him through. By then it won't matter if he realises you are behind him – although if he is a bad as you say he is, he probably won't even notice you. We have a couple of officers waiting. They have been liaising with the French police on duty. Remind me again of your registration and make and colour so that our chaps let you through".

"Will do. See you in Folkstone or Dover".

"I won't be there, the Kent police are waiting to pick him up".

Rory followed James through France, only getting right behind him as they approached the entrance to the railway station, where as the inspector had said they were directed round to the front of the queue. If James was surprised only he knew.

As they disembarked from the train, Rory could see a group of British policemen, several police cars and a low loader ready to collect James's car. He waited until the police had helped James into one of their cars before getting out to speak to them.

"I'm on my way home", said Rory. Do what you can to try and find out if he knows where the little boy is".

"We will, Sir. Thank you for your help in getting him here".

Chapter 20

Everyone concerned in the hunt for Hugo had experienced a terrible night, especially James because the questioning had gone on relentlessly. It soon became obvious that Keith was right, and James didn't actually know where Hugo was being held, but he certainly knew far more than he would admit.

"Where's the boy?"

"I don't know!"

"Where was he taken?"

"I don't know, I honestly don't know", said James in desperation,

"You wouldn't know the meaning of honesty, Mr Brierly. Tell me where your brother took him?"

"Please believe me. I don't know. I would tell you if I did. He was always sneaky and devious".

"Quick to blame someone else".

"I swear I had nothing to do with the kidnap. It wasn't me who demanded £3 million".

The special branch man said nothing. Nobody had mentioned the amount of the ransom. 'Got you', he thought, and glanced towards his colleague who was taking down everything, alongside a machine taping every word.

The policeman conducting the interview swiftly changed the subject.

"We found a passport in amongst your papers in the boot of your car. How do you explain the photo in the passport. You, or what was you until what you say was a car crash did to you, but how come the name is different, Mr Brierly?"

The doctor who had briefly examined him said that the injuries were not conducive with a car crash – it certainly looked more like somebody had violently taken it out of him.

James said nothing.

"Come on Mr Brierly, where did you get it? Who supplied it? What about the airline ticket? Were you planning to fly out to Rio on Monday, after you'd collected the ransom?"

"I didn't have anything to do with it. It was my brother Bernard's idea. He suggested it and we were going to share the money. He's always bullied me, It wasn't my fault!"

"Not only a liar, but a coward as well".

The phone went and the man in charge left the room to answer it. The inspector was on the other end, "How's it going?"

"Badly, I'm afraid, the man is a compulsive liar, but he's so experienced at lying, that we are having one hell of a time tripping him up. He did let it out that he knew how much the ransom is. We've got that on tape. We've had a piece of luck though. When we really searched his car and personal belongings, we came across definite proof that he was planning to leave the country, or France, anyway. He had, hidden in amongst car document papers, another passport. It contained a photograph of him, but with a completely different name. Along with it was an airline ticket from Zurich to Rio in South America. Mr James Brierly was planning to skip Europe!"

"We need to find out where he got that passport."

"We're on to that sir. I am convinced we'll break him".

"He wasn't going to take the blame, he was leaving that to his brother Bernard. I guess he was going to grab all the money and scarper", answered the inspector.

"If I might ask sir, is there any news of where the child is?"

"No, not yet. I'm sure something will come up soon. Keep trying to break him down. There's got to be something he knows".

James continued to argue that it had nothing to do with any kidnap, that it was to do with gambling debts, which he confessed to during the night. He also owned up to the fact that there never been a car accident, he *had* been beaten up, but he wouldn't tell who had been responsible, merely that he had some gambling debts.

Chapter 21

ory went straight to the manor house, where he met up with Alison and Helen, who was extremely subdued.

"We've only got a day before they hurt my son, Rory". Rory glanced at Alison.

"She's been counting down the hours. All we can do is to try and reassure her. Tell us what happened while you were away".

"I crossed over as you know and went directly to Maligny although I didn't go straight to James's cottage – I went next door instead, to his neighbour's house. They have a driveway entrance a little further up the road and so I pulled in there. Both Marie and Louis were in the garden and as I approached them, I knew Marie was about to call out, but I managed to signal to her to keep quiet. The three of us went into her 'salon' where we could talk with no chance of James hearing anything. The first thing I asked was whether James's son Hugo was staying with him. Marie looked puzzled but shook her head".

"No, only Christiane. How long she will last the whole village is asking. He's a bad man that James. Rory, I ask why you thought the child would be here?"

"It's not a very nice story, and I will have to ask you not to repeat it, at least until Hugo is found. You remember Helen and the children?"

"But of course. She was always very polite, and we often talked over our wall. She told me all about her father and his books and films and we laughed about the strange neighbours on the corner opposite. That husband James, didn't deserve her, it was known that when she was staying here in the cottage, he would say he was going to the bar in the village, when the whole village knew he was going round to see Christiane – that was before her mother died and then after Helen stopped coming to France, Christiane moved in with him. She made a very big mistake everyone says".

Marie paused and Rory was able to carry on.

"We believe he has been involved with the kidnap of his son. That is why I am here to check up on him".

Both Marie and Louis showed how shocked they were by the expressions on their faces. Finally, it was Marie who spoke, she was always the most verbally expressive of the pair. All she could say was 'Merde'.

Anyway, I eventually made my escape, collected my car and parked it outside James's house as though I had just arrived.

"James was at home and offered me a bed. I knew then that Hugo wasn't there, but when James went down to the boulangerie I had a chance to have a good look around and there was no sign Hugo had ever been there. So that fooled me, I was so convinced I'd find him there. I made an excuse to stay on, said I was over to buy wine for a customer".

He continued, "I made the acquaintance of his live-in girlfriend, although after a huge row she moved out the next day. I have since had a long chat with her, and as Colin suggested, she opened up. He'd actually told her he had organised the kidnap so that Helen would pay up. When she questioned him about where he'd been on Sunday and not getting back until Monday morning, he said he'd driven through France to meet up with Bernard and Hugo. She didn't believe him and suggested he'd gone to visit some other woman. I think she was right".

Helen, looking dazed, gave the impression it wasn't news to her. He'd been like this ever since she'd known him

Alison was anxious to hear what happened next.

"Colin told me they were going to try encouraging James to come back to England. They didn't want to arrest him in France – extradition and all that. He said he'd planned to involve Keith in this. Anyway, he asked me to stay on and follow James. I gave him all of James's details, car type, number plate and then when we got close to Calais, the crossing times".

Rory continued, "We came through the tunnel to meet up with the police. They put James into the police car, and the car on to a low loader. I spoke briefly to Colin and told him I was coming here. By the way Alison, what news on the money?"

"We haven't got it all, about £1,500,000. We are hoping they will accept this – maybe with the confirmation we can get the rest next week. I am ready to transfer it as soon as they tell us where to. When the call comes, I am planning to answer the phone. Helen isn't up to it. Our voices are similar so I don't think they will guess".

Alison continued, "You mentioned James had been beaten up. What happened?"

"We don't really know. Marie and Louis, his neighbours, saw a couple of men arrive – about 8.30pm they think. Marie looked over the wall and saw the men push their way into the house and slam the door behind them. She heard shouting and then someone, presumably James, screaming. She said she and Louis didn't really care; James deserved everything he got".

"Then what happened", asked Alison.

"I was told by Colin that he spoke to Keith and asked him to make a call to James and to stress the urgency of James's return".

"Do you know what Colin asked him to say?"

"I understand Colin told him to tell James that Keith was going solo – that he was planning to demand the money and keep it for himself".

"Whoa, that would upset him!"

"There were some other things as well. But I can't remember what".

Later Rory, when Helen left the room briefly, told Alison that James was told by Keith that Bernard was prepared kill Hugo, but neither Colin or he believed it was true.

"I couldn't tell you this in front of Helen".

"Thank goodness you didn't. I think it would have pushed her completely over the top.

Rory continued his story, "Colin asked me to stay on and find out as much as I could. James is definitely involved with the kidnap, along with his brother Bernard. As far as we know, Keith, the other brother is co-operating and helping the police as much as he can, but he doesn't know where Bernard and Hugo could be".

Rory continued, "I talked to his French girlfriend, at least she was his live-in girlfriend until a couple of days ago. They had a big falling out, especially when he blurted out he'd asked his brother to kidnap Hugo and demand £3 million from his former wife, Helen. That made her so mad she dumped him immediately. What we don't know is what he was doing on Sunday and Monday morning. He told Christiane he'd gone to meet Bernard and Hugo, but none of us believe that. I suspect Christiane is right and he had a liaison with somebody else's wife!"

Alison moved over to sit beside Helen and took her sister's hand.

"Ali, we've only got a day before they take action", said Helen in an anguished voice.

"It's alright Sis, the police will find him. We've got great faith in Colin".

Rory asked, "How about the money?"

It was Alison who answered, "We've got £1.5 million ready to be transferred. We are working on getting more, but we are hoping they'll accept the lower amount. When, if the call comes in, I will answer it. My voice is very similar to Helen's and I'll pretend I am her".

"I'll be here right beside you Ali", Rory added.

At that moment the phone went and everyone jumped. Alison slowly lifted the phone to her ear.

"Hello", but instead of the kidnapper, it was Colin and he sounded upbeat.

"Alison, we've got another breakthrough we think". Alison held her breath while giving a thumb signal to Rory and turning the phone to speaker volume so that he could listen in as well.

"We had another conversation with Keith, that was while we were explaining what we wanted him to say in his phone call to James. Keith said he didn't know what is was, but he'd suddenly remembered roughly where the cottage is that Keith might have taken Hugo. He says he vaguely remembers staying on a farm somewhere near the town of Llandrindod Wells".

Helen sat up, "I vaguely remember my father saying something about a farm near there, but I can't remember what or why".

Colin who could hear them joined in, "That all makes sense. It could well have been when he was married to his first wife, mother of Bernard and Keith. He wasn't James's father. He came along after his first wife re-married".

Helen stiffened. She now knew about her father's first marriage and her two half-brothers, but she still hadn't come to terms with it.

Rory entered the conversation and asked Colin if he'd spoken to Keith about phoning James.

"Yes I did. First of all he hadn't heard from either Keith or James, and I can tell you that he's in a dreadful state. Says he feels so responsible and is beating himself up for not contacting us when Keith and Hugo stayed overnight. The poor man will do anything he can to help".

"I can't call him a 'poor man", interrupted Alison, with more than a touch of derision.

The inspector continued. "I asked him to have another go at both of them. Bernard still isn't answering, but Keith finally got through to James. This would have been the morning after he had the two visitors. I have since asked Keith about who they might have been and the only thing he can think of was something to do the James's gambling debts".

The inspector went on, "Keith told him, untruthfully, that he'd spoken to Bernard, who was keeping as far away from everyone, especially James, as possible. Bernard said he was fed up with James ordering the two of them around, and that he didn't trust James to share out the money – in fact he was pretty sure James would collect the cash and drop both his half-brothers in the thick of it, while denying having anything to do with the kidnap. How could he have been involved while he was on holiday in France? Anyway Keith told him Bernard was planning to take the lot".

"Whoa, that would upset him", remarked Alison.

"Yes that answers a few questions. I know James was in a bad place when I dropped by on Wednesday afternoon. I put it down to Christiane walking out, but if he'd spoken to Keith, it could have been that. I remember him saying he might be going away for a few days".

"I may be guessing, but was it that evening – Wednesday evening, he had his run-in with the two English guys?"

"Yes, it must have been because on Thursday Mr Brierly headed back over here and he was in bad shape".

After the phone conversation between the inspector and Helen and her family, Colin told them he was about to complete the interrogation with James and would then be heading back to the manor.

Chapter 22

ernard didn't sleep well either. Every small sound made his nerves jangle. A mouse or a rat, scurrying behind a stack of wood in the corner of the room, made him think somebody was trying to get in. He cursed himself for being such a fool as to have got involved with this stupid business. How had he been conned by that miserable little twerp? Oh yes, James had wound him up all right with the talk of a million quid.

"We'll be able to travel the world," he'd said, "and visit all the places you've ever wanted to see. We will get the money, meet up and travel together. There are places like the Grand Canyon and Las Vegas just waiting for us!"

But now as Bernard lay on the hard floor, he wondered if James had again been manipulating him and he felt very sorry for himself. God, he felt old!

He turned over thinking about what he would do. First of all, he needed to get in touch with James. He was really worried that he hadn't been able to raise him. If he couldn't get James, then he would phone Helen and pass on the message about the Swiss Bank account, which James had opened ready to receive the £3 million. He'd said it was a good idea to transfer the money to Switzerland.

They'd risen early, he and Hugo and had breakfast. Hugo was really excited about seeing his mum again later that day. And just after eight he tried to call James again but no one answered the phone. Before he phoned Helen, he decided to remove all evidence of their stay.

It took longer than Bernard thought it would to get things sorted out. He didn't want to take their rubbish with them so he dug a hole to bury the tin cans, useless boxes and other waste. He planned to take Hugo with him in his car to Conway. He'd be glad to get away now. It had been fun renewing his memories of the area, but after catching a glimpse of someone across the fields, probably the farmer, he felt trapped.

It was time to call Helen again and tell her what to do with the money.

Alison picked up the phone, conscious that she must pretend she was Helen. "Hallo, Helen Brierly here," she said, hoping it wasn't one of Helen's friends.

"Just listen, and do as I tell you", replied Bernard as he held the recording of Hugo crying up to his phone.

"Who is it? Who's calling?" Alison asked, feeling herself trembling with fear.

"Never you mind. Just write down this number. This is the number of the bank account for you to transfer the money into."

"Hold on a minute while I grab a pen. We've only managed to get £1.5 million. We can get the rest next week, but please, please let Hugo go now".

There was a brief pause as if the kidnapper was thinking.

"Ok that will have to do. Hurry up will you! Right – put this down and make sure the money gets into this account. I will be checking with the bank at 4.30 this afternoon, and if you haven't done what I've said, you won't see the boy again! Understand! *No money – no son!*" and he immediately hung up hoping he'd put 'the fear of God' into her!

Alison was shaking when Rory had been standing near her, and although he couldn't hear what Bernard had said, he knew it had been enough to upset Alison.

"That was him, he played a recording of Hugo crying!" she said. "He told me to get Helen to transfer the money into a Swiss Bank account, but I think he made a mistake – it was an English bank account number, definitely not Swiss!"

Rory exploded, "James! He's planned all this! Bernard isn't bright enough. I hate James for what he's doing to his family – including Bernard and Keith. I know they've done wrong, but, I understand from Keith that James has always had them under his thumb."

"What do we do now?", asked Alison

"Well obviously we need to let Helen and the accountant know, then take advice from there on. Colin is on his way here, so we can tell him when he arrives."

Alison phoned the accountant who told them to leave transferring the money until as late as possible. The accountant suggested he'd have a word with the bank to tell them to be prepared to stop the payment at the last minute.

Alison replied, "We said we can only get £1.5 million by this afternoon – he hesitated and then agreed to take that".

She turned back and spoke to her husband, "I've been thinking about where they might be and I don't think it is local, I don't know if you remember dad's neighbour, Sir Edwin Stone? He and dad were great friends, Ed owned and flew his own helicopter, the two of them often went to York Races or the British Grand Prix. While you were heading back here, I called Ed and asked him if he was still flying himself around, he was quite a bit younger than dad, and he said yes. I told him about Hugo – I know we have to be so careful, but as we don't know where the kidnapper took him, I thought we might need some sort of transport to get us there quickly, and time is running out. He sounded very angry about the kidnapping and said of course he would make himself available. I said it might be today. He'll get the helicopter prepared and will bring it over to the big field we used as a car park on Sunday".

"Well done Ali, great thinking. Think Colin will be here in a few minutes".

Chapter 23

nspector Jarvis was worried. He'd told Helen the police were sure they would find Hugo, but as the hours went by, he was becoming increasingly less hopeful. They had put out feelers to every police force throughout the country and nothing had turned up.

"Where the bloody hell is the man?" the inspector exclaimed out loud.

"Sorry guv, what did you say?" asked the startled policeman driving the car.

The inspector was deep in thought and didn't reply.

Minutes ticked by – and still nothing.

"We need a break son – a little bit of luck" said the inspector to the young constable.

Within minutes, he was to get that piece of luck.

Constable Dai Thomas was passing his police station that morning at about 10.30 am, and although he wasn't due on duty until noon, he'd been thinking about hearing the voice of a child. He didn't think anymore about it. Just somebody camping, he thought, On impulse, he decided to look through a broken window on the side of the barn, but decided it must be OK. He could only see the side of car so couldn't get the number.

P.C. Paul Chason looked up and said, "Where the hell have you been Dai? We've searched all over the place for you!"

"Why? I'm not due on duty until noon today!"

"Because we need everybody in – we've got a big job on. Where were you anyway? We tried your home number; we tried your mum's, but she didn't know. Where did you go?"

P.C. Thomas had the grace to turn red. "Visiting a lady friend," he said sheepishly.

"What? So her husband's out of town is he?"

"Yes, as a matter of fact he is – over in America. Anyway, what's going on?" Dai asked his mate.

"It's the kidnap of that little boy."

"What little boy? What's happened?"

"An inspector from England, thinks that the kid is being held in a ruined cottage somewhere around these parts – but nobody seems to know exactly where. One of his contacts seems to have remembered having a holiday in this area, can't remember anything more".

Dai Thomas slowly said, "I think *I* know where."

"You – what? You know where the kid is, and you haven't told anyone!"

"Well, I didn't know a kid was missing. When did it happen?"

"I guess the boy was taken last Sunday and everybody's been looking for him ever since, but he could be in this area. What are you doing here, anyway, if you didn't realise you were needed."

"I met up with 'old man Morgan' – you know? He lives at Bryn Farm. I met him at the pub last night and he told me an odd story about this man and a little boy staying in a tumble down cottage Dick Morgan owns. Mr Morgan was curious because he saw some smoke coming out of the chimney. Anyway he decides to go and have a nosy around. He says he went across his ten acre field and into a bit of wood where he could look down and sees an old man and a kid. He says he was a bit feared to go any closer – wasn't sure if they were gypsies or summurt. He said he had a creep around when the man and the kid go into the kitchen, so he thinks he'll check out one of the barns – the one a bit further away from the old derelict cottage. It were about 100 yards from the cottage, he could see through from the back where the boards have come away that there was a car hidden inside. It was too dark to see what sort of car or its number plate. He didn't like to go round to the front of the building in case he was seen. So, Mr Morgan goes back towards his farmhouse and finds one of his cows has got stuck in a ditch and by the time he'd got it out, he'd forgotten about the car.".

Two of the unknown policemen were listening in. One of them called out, "Get the inspector on the phone –*now!* We think we've made a break!"

"Right, Sarge!"

The Sergeant came over to P.C. Thomas and asked, "Where exactly is this cottage?"

"It's across the field in a bit of a wood. I'd have to ask old Dick Morgan."

Sergeant Paul Jones was already looking up the number for the Morgan's of Bryn Farm.

"Hell, there are a lot of Morgan's in the book", he commented. "Ah, here it is."

P.C. Thomas dialled the number as Paul called it out to him. The phone rang and rang. Dai was about to hang up when a breathless voice answered it.

"Hallo"

"Hallo. Is that Mrs Morgan?"

"That's right – yes," she answered.

"Is your husband there, Mrs Morgan?" the policeman asked.

"No, he's away up on the Common, above Peny-bont," she replied, trying to get her breath back. "Sorry, I was out collecting the eggs when I heard the phone ringing and I just came running across the yard.

Anyway, Mr Morgan got a phone call saying it looked like one of his sheep was caught in a bramble, and he went off after it."

"Do you know when he'll be back, Mrs Morgan?"

"Not 'till dinner time, I expect."

The Sergeant was nudging him, "Ask her if she knows where the cottage is."

"Right Sir…. Mrs Morgan, did your husband tell you all about the man and a little boy in your old cottage?"

"He did that. Said as he thought it was queer. But he said he told Dai all about it in the pub last night".

Dai nodded, "Yes. Yes he did. Could you tell us where the cottage is, Mrs Morgan?"

"Well, it's across the fields from here - best you wait until Dick gets back."

"Does Dick have a mobile phone?"

"No – he doesn't hold with them newfangled things."

"Could you hold on a minute, Mrs Morgan?"

"Yes, I'll do that for you, Dai."

The P.C. turned to the others and asked, "What shall I do now? Seems like the old man is out somewhere, looking for a sheep, and Mrs Morgan says the cottage is across the fields."

"Ask her if anyone heading for the ruined cottage would have to come past their house to get to the main road."

P.C. Thomas duly asked the question of Mrs Morgan.

"No, she says. If it is the old barn she thinks it is, there's a track that comes out further down the main road."

"Right then, tell her you'll be on your way up, but if her husband gets home before you get there, make sure he stays and doesn't go off somewhere else. Tell her it's *very* important!"

"OK sir, I'll do that. Do you want me to go there straight away, or should I go and get into uniform?"

"No, hang on until we've had a talk to the English inspector, to see what he wants us to do."

P.C. Dai Thomas turned back to the phone and spoke again to Mrs Morgan to explain what had been discussed at the police station. "It's OK sarge, she says she'll keep him there."

One of the Special Branch policemen had been talking to Inspector Jarvis. When the call came through, the inspector was sitting staring at a cup of cold coffee, hardly listening and wondering what to do next. They had contacted every local police station for miles and nobody knew anything. In fact, he was beginning to wonder whether he'd been wise to listen to Keith's instincts. Perhaps her son had been taken somewhere completely different. Scotland, perhaps?

The phone rang, and one of the local men picked it up. "It's for you, inspector."

"Thanks," he said, in a dispirited tone.

"Hallo inspector, it's, Mike Cooper here."

"Hallo Mike. What's new?"

"We think we've found him. The little boy."

"What?" shouted the Colin Jarvis. "Where, where is he? Have you got him there?"

"No, but we believe we've located the cottage, Sir. One of the local farmers was having a chat to a P.C. from this station, in the pub last night. He, the farmer, mentioned that he'd seen some smoke coming from a semi-derelict cottage on his land. When he investigated, he saw an old man with a small boy.

Anyway he did a bit of snooping and discovered a car hidden in a disused barn about a 100 yards from the cottage.

He said he didn't like to go any closer and was heading home to get his shotgun when he found his cow stuck in the mud in a ditch. Anyway, by the time Dai Morgan had been home and got his tractor out and some gear to pull the cow out, he'd forgotten all about the old man and the boy.

"OK, slow down a bit Mike. You said you'd located the cottage. Nobody's been there yet, have they?"

"No, only the old farmer, who walked past there yesterday, I understand."

"Right – now you said this P.C. Thomas got the information last night. Why didn't he act on it before?"

"He's been off duty - I gather he was due to come on at noon today and just happened to pop in early."

"I thought each station was contacting their uniformed staff, and asking them to come in early this morning to help in the search."

"That's right, inspector. They tried to contact him, but he wasn't at his own home – he's a bachelor, you see. And he wasn't at his mum's."

"Where was he then?"

"It seems he was visiting a girlfriend. He doesn't like advertising the fact, in case it gets back to the husband, but that's why the sergeant here, had no way of locating him!"

"Oh, my God! Well anyway, he's in now. As soon as you find out exactly where the old cottage and barn is, get someone back down there and get the number on the number plate asap; and the colour. If it is a silver Mondeo as I think it maybe, we already know its number. But we still need to run it through the DVLA."

"Look, tell me where you are and I'll get back to you as soon as possible. I'm in Wiltshire at the moment but have a helicopter on stand-by. Oh, and give me the telephone number there – I'll call you on my mobile and you can fill me in on what's happening. I don't have to tell you to keep everything as secret as possible. I don't want our suspect to guess we are on to him".

"Right Sir", and the lead policeman on the case gave him the information he needed and they hung up.

On the way over to the manor where Helen and the family were all waiting for news, Inspector Jarvis made a quick call to Helen and Rory. He knew Helen was almost at the end of her tether and hoped the news that at long last they were getting somewhere, would help her.

Rory answered the phone in Helen's room. Colin Jarvis quickly gave him the brief information. He heard Rory turn to Helen and say, "Helen, it's good news – they think they've found where Hugo is being held."

Almost before he could finish, Helen came on the phone, "Colin it is true? Have you found him?" she cried out, half laughing, half crying.

"Helen, we believe we've found where he's being held – but no, we haven't been to the cottage ."

"I'm coming with you!" she said. "Where are you now? We'll come there!"

"I'm heading towards you. Its great news about your father's neighbour with the helicopter. Please can you ask him to be ready to go as soon as I arrive".

"Oh, please Colin, please let me come with you? Hugo might be frightened of seeing strangers coming at him".

"Yes, I want both you and Rory to come. Be as quick as you can. Grab some clothes for you and Hugo and anything else you can think of. I'll bring the directions with me for your helicopter neighbour to head straight there – allowing for congested airspace of course. But if he's as experienced as you say he is, he'll be able to navigate without too many problems. The only thing I will say is that you won't be able to approach the cottage because it could be dangerous".

"Yes, I understand. Oh Colin, do you think Hugo is OK?"

"As his 'uncle' doesn't know we have found them, everything should be fine. But time is vital and I don't want to waste any more. Where is the helicopter at the manor".

"In the field where all the cars were parked on Sunday".

When Inspector Colin Jarvis arrived he found both Helen and Rory standing beside the helicopter, with Sir Edwin Stone. Helen had a small bag with a few things in it and all four of them quickly climbed into the chopper.

Colin offered to let Helen sit up front with the pilot but after thanking him she said she preferred to sit next to Rory behind them. The inspector hoped she might doze off while they were travelling because he was shocked at how weary she looked. She didn't go to sleep, in fact. Helen had so many questions she wanted to ask, but after the first minute, she remembered how noisy and difficult it was to make any reasonable conversation so she just sat back and waited until they arrived at their destination.

Upon climbing into the aircraft the inspector handed over the map and directions for the destination and the pilot spent a few minutes logging in the details. Helen was already shaking again, but knew she had to try and be patient while Ed Stone made his final checks before lifting off and heading westwards, before turning north and following the M5 for a while, and then turning west again towards Llandrindod Wells.

During the flight the pilot constantly changed his settings as he picked up one radio beacon after another and they could all hear the sounds of pilots in other aircraft as they navigated into different airports en route. The inspector had thought about what he should say to Sir Ed. Rory had told him Ali had given him an outline about the kidnapping, and although Colin believed he could totally trust him, but until the child was safe, they had to be careful nothing got out to the press and thus warn the kidnapper, although he thought this was unlikely. With James safely locked up in a police cell, Keith helping the police and Bernard holed up somewhere remote.

He smiled to himself when he thought about Keith's information as to where he thought Bernard might have taken Hugo. According to Sergeant Andy Boon, Keith had searched maps of Wales to see if anything triggered off a memory. It was only when Keith noticed the name of a town that he called out 'Landiddy' – that's it! Andy was a bit surprised to see him pointing at Llandrindod Wells, but Keith told him he hadn't been able to pronounce the name when he was little and so called it 'Landiddy' at which his mother and Bernard had laughed at him.

Pressure was building up again in Inspector Jarvis's head. He felt they were nearing the end of the case – they had to be, because they only had five hours before the deadline and so every minute seemed to race past so quickly, and he found himself saying a silent prayer they had actually found the right area.

Helen was quiet as they progressed towards their destination and it was only after they flew over the border into Wales that she began frantically scanning the ground beneath the helicopter, looking out for anywhere that might conceal Hugo. Had she but known it, they almost passed over the spot and if she'd looked down through a little wooded area, she might have noticed a small boy looking up and waving to the helicopter as it flew overhead.

Inspector Jarvis told Sir Ed Stone he didn't want the aircraft to land anywhere close to the cottage and so, after some discussion with someone knowledgeable about the area near Llandrindod Wells, they agreed he should land on the edge of the golf course belonging to a hotel just outside the town.

After further discussion, the inspector arranged for a car to pick him up to take him to the temporary headquarters of the inquiry and that Rory and Helen, along with the pilot, should go into the hotel for a coffee and sandwiches.

"I couldn't eat anything", said Helen, "it would make me sick".

"Please try. You'll need your strength". Colin refrained from saying when we find Hugo safe and well. "I will have a car standing by to pick you both up as soon as I know where we are up to".

"Have they found Hugo yet?", she asked anxiously.

"We haven't actually seen him yet, but we believe he is in the ruined cottage with Bernard".

"Oh Colin, I don't know how long I can go on! If only he would call again asking for the money, I'd send it straight away so that he'd release Hugo".

"I know. I'm getting some really good reports from the local police. They believe they have found him. So please stay here with Rory and someone will collect you shortly".

The inspector could understand her desire to be at the cottage when they surrounded it – but he hadn't told her he'd have armed officers with him, and it might be dangerous.

As he joined his Welsh colleagues, orders began flying around

Inspector Jarvis called Mike Cooper to find out what was happening. "Hi, Mike. Any more news?"

"Well, one thing, Sir. We've heard from Swansea. The car belongs to a car hire firm in Wiltshire. We've been in touch with them and they confirm it was leased out to a Mr Bernard Smith on Monday morning

"That's it – we've got him!" almost shouted the inspector.

Mike told him about the farmer's wife and that Dai Thomas had gone up to the farm to wait for Dick Morgan, the farmer, to come back from the Common.

"I understand that Mr Smith would have to come out by a farm track on to the main road and so I've sent a car up there to block the exit."

"Good. Well done. Are there any other ways he could leave the cottage?"

"Only by foot, I believe, but we're not actually sure exactly where the cottage is. It's only from something Mrs Morgan said, that we understand it's completely off the beaten track."

When the inspector arrived at the small police station, he found an air of excitement. Dai Thomas was waiting to accompany him to the farm.

"Well done, constable. It's a pity we didn't hear from you sooner. I hope your married girlfriend was worth it!" he said with a smile, as he watched the constable go red.

"Yes, sir," replied P.C. Thomas. "You'll be wanting me to get back up to Bryn Farm now, will you Sir?"

"That's the place where your farmer friend lives, is it?"

"That's right, Sir."

"OK Constable. Off you go. Give the directions to my driver will you, because I'll be following you up shortly."

P.C. Thomas made his escape. He knew he would be teased by his colleagues, so he was anxious to get away.

Inspector Jarvis went over to talk to Mike Cooper. The armed officers were on their way and would be heading to the farm to meet up with the inspector and get their orders, as and when, the inspector knew where they were heading.

Before the inspector had left for the farm, Helen arrived with Rory. She was about to give the inspector a big hug, when he went forward, took her hand and said, "Hallo, Mrs Brierly." She realised at once that he was with his colleagues, and professionalism and formality had to be preserved.

"Oh, Colin, I'm so happy you've found him!"

Inspector Jarvis took both of her hands, and oblivious to the other people in the room, gently said, "We know where he has been kept during the week. What we don't know, is if he's still there, Helen. The car is still in the barn, so unless Bernard has walked out of there, we are sure we will find them. We are all very hopeful of finding Hugo safe and well, but until we get to the cottage, we won't know if Mr Bernard Smith has left or not. We know he was there early this morning, but so far, today, we are completely in the dark."

"He must be there, Colin. I don't know what I'll do if it is not him or he's gone! I know I'll go mad!"

Inspector Colin Jarvis abandoned all his training about getting involved and took her in his arms and said, "Helen, hold on for a little while longer – I really feel it is Hugo and he will be OK. Just hang on. We've absolutely no evidence that Mr Smith has ever committed any violent act and so we have to believe he's been manipulated by your husband, James."

Helen wept silently into his shoulder.

"Look, Helen, I have to go. Why don't you stay here until we have some news?"

"No! I can't. I *must* be there and know what's going on!"

"I can't let you come with us. But – perhaps Rory could take you somewhere along the main road, near to where the track goes to the cottage. By the way – is Ed Stone, your helicopter pilot still around?" Helen said he was and gave the inspector his mobile number.

Inspector Jarvis turned to Rory, "Will you check with your wife and ask her if she has heard anything. I must be on my way, we've only got four and a half hours before the deadline".

"Thanks Helen – now, I must go. One of the coppers here will direct you where to go when we know a bit more."

She looked a bit doubtful, the inspector seeing this said, "I promise".

As he left he thought about the use he might have to make of the helicopter. He was hoping it wouldn't be needed to ferry anyone to the local hospital, but it would be the quickest way to get someone out from the remote area the cottage was in.

Helen looked lost after the inspector left. One of the local policemen came over to her to ask her if she'd like a cup of tea or coffee.

"Coffee, please. Black, no sugar, thank you."

"And you, sir? The same policeman asked, turning to Rory.

"Coffee, please, with milk and one sugar."

Rory led Helen to a couple of chairs at one side of the room. "Helen, they're doing everything they can. We're in their hands now. I'm sure Colin will let us know as soon as anything happens," he said gently.

"I know Rory. It was just that I thought we'd found him, and that he'd be here when we arrived. But he's not! We've still got to wait. When I think of James I feel such anger and hatred for him. If he were here right now, I swear I'd kill him!" she exclaimed.

"I feel exactly the same. By the way, I called Ali. She's OK now, and the children are having a great time. Amy seems happy to be in our home again and was demanding they take their lunch up into the tree house. Ali agreed, of course. She says it's hard to stay miserable with that foursome around."

Helen smiled at the thought of her daughter and her cousins charging round the garden. She wondered what Alison would give them for supper.

Inspector Jarvis left the police station to follow P.C. Dai Thomas up to Bryn Farm. He had arranged for his team of armed police to meet him there. On the way, he phoned Sir Ed Stone, Helen's friendly pilot, and asked him to stand by. Ed offered to fly over straight away, but the inspector declined, because it might forewarn the kidnapper – and that was the last thing he wanted to do.

At the farm, Mr Morgan had just arrived back from sorting out his sheep. He was surprised to find Dai Thomas waiting for him.

"Hallo Dai. Find out anything about that car, have you?"

"Aye – I have, and, about that old man at the cottage. The boy is not his grandson, at all, look you. He's been kidnapped and is being held to ransom."

"What?" Mr Morgan, exclaimed. "Eh, Dai. I wish I'd said something sooner. I knew back on Monday someone was in the cottage, but I've been so busy, I haven't had time to come and tell anybody!"

"Well, thank goodness you told me last night. We've got coppers from all over the country – some of them are on their way up here now, so I've got to ask you to stay here and guide them to the cottage."

The old man appeared to have aged instantly – so shocked was he by what he'd just heard. "Right, I'll do that. I'll just pop in and tell the missus what's going on. I'll be straight out again don't you fear."

"Off you go then," the constable said. "Don't be long, I think I've just heard the sound of a car coming. It'll be the inspector, I guess."

Two minutes later, the old man came out of the farmhouse at the same time as Inspector Jarvis was driven into the yard, followed by a police van, which contained the six armed officers.

Dai Thomas brought old Mr Morgan over to introduce him to the inspector.

Mr Morgan said how sorry he was that he hadn't said anything sooner about the cottage, though the inspector privately agreed with him, he just replied that he was glad he had told P.C. Thomas.

"Where is the cottage, Mr Morgan?"

The old man pointed down towards what looked like a bit of woodland in the corner of a couple of big fields. "It's down there, beyond the 'ten acre'," he answered.

"What's the best way to approach it? I'd like to send my men down from different directions so we can surround it – but I'd like them to get there without being seen."

"Well, you could go down across the 'ten acre'. You couldn't be seen from the cottage because the field is side on and none of the windows face that way. The hedges are quite high and there's a gate at the bottom end. It's a bit overgrown near the cottage, but you can get through."

"That's fine. I'll send a couple of my men that way. I think I'd better get you, Constable Thomas, to take two of them round to where the track comes out on to the road, if you don't mind. I'll brief you in a moment. And, the other two, perhaps down that field to the right. It should come out somewhere near the cottage, I guess."

"Aye, it does," said the old farmer, "But it's a bit exposed that way – comes out right in front of the cottage. If they go one more field over that way, they would be out of sight – and there's a stile near the end of that hedge."

"OK. Thanks – we'll do that."

"I could lead them round, if you like."

"Fine, if you would show them the way, but you mustn't go too close. When they can see the stile, you stop and come back here."

Mr Morgan nodded.

Inspector Jarvis divided his marksmen into three pairs. "Willis you and Rimmer – go with Mr Morgan. Stockton and Lewis – take the 'ten acre' field. Be careful – we don't know if he is armed or not. I'll follow you down shortly. Now constable, take Prentice and McDonald back to the track entrance."

Willis and Rimmer had already disappeared round behind the big hay barn at one end of the yard, while Stockton and Lewes were heading in the opposite direction.

The inspector turned back to Prentice and McDonald. "Make your way up the track, bearing in mind that Mr Smith may well be coming out in his car. Oh, and by the way, there should be a big barn somewhere along there. Check and see if there is a car in it or not. Let me know what you find – in that way I'll know if Mr Smith is still around, or whether or not we are wasting our time here."

The two armed policemen nodded briefly and said a curt, "Yes, Sir" as they turned to go off with P.C. Thomas.

"One more thing," called out the inspector. "Mrs Brierly, the boy's mother, will be down on the road. Please ask her to stay there. I do *not* want her coming with you, or following you – is that understood?"

"Yes, Sir," they replied, and were gone.

"What would you like me to do?" asked the driver who had brought the inspector to the farm.

"I think you'd better follow P.C. Thomas round to the road. I imagine I'll come out that way. But you'd better wait until I hear from Prentice and McDonald about the car. If it's already gone, I'll need a ride back to H.Q. I can't help telling you though – I hope to God it's still there!"

At that moment, Mrs Morgan appeared with two mugs of tea for them, which they gratefully accepted.

Unaware that the net was closing in, Bernard and Hugo had taken the last things to the car and when Uncle Bernard was satisfied he told Hugo to get onto the back seat and lie down.

"I just want to do a last check at the cottage. I won't be long," he said.

Hugo did as he was told. It was warm and dark in the car still hidden in the barn. The seat was certainly more comfortable than the wooden floor of the cottage. Hugo began to doze off, which was why he didn't hear anyone go past the semi-derelict building.

Bernard made his way, for one last time, back to the cottage. Once there, he tried James again, but still no reply. Perhaps James's mobile is out of action, he thought. Somehow he'd have to find a way to contact him when he got to the boat.

Bernard thought about whether anyone would link him with the cottage, and at that moment he made his fatal mistake. On the spur of the moment he decided to set the cottage on fire – to burn it down. It would burn easily as there was so much dry wood stored in it.

Remembering his scout days he carefully collected some small twigs and made a wigwam with them around dry leaves he pulled off some of the bigger branches. Larger sticks were added until he had built a sizeable bonfire. Unknown to him, the net was closing in rapidly.

The minutes stretched away. Ten – fifteen – and, then suddenly the inspector's radio receiver, burst into life.

"It's McDonald here, Sir."

"Thank God for that – I thought you'd got lost."

"We've made our way up the track, Sir, towards that cottage. We've found the old barns. We haven't been in, but we could see through a broken door – there's a car in there, all right."

"Great! Don't waste time checking it out now. Make your way towards the cottage. I'll let the others know our quarry is still there. Be very careful – don't forget there's an eight year old boy in the cottage, whose mother loves him very much indeed."

"Yes, sir. We're on our way now."

The inspector contacted the other two pairs. Willis and Rimmer were already in place near the stile and old Mr Morgan was on his way back to the farm, they said.

"Can you see anything from where you are?"

"No, only a glimpse of the cottage. There's a stream, which runs through here and seems to go past the front of the building."

"OK. Stay where you are until I give you the order to move."

"Right, Sir."

Stockton and Lewes were also in place.

"Very overgrown, Sir. We're about one hundred yards away but the bushes are so thick, we can only just see the cottage."

"OK – stay where you are. I'm on my way."

Everybody waited in silence. The tension was becoming unbearable. The armed policemen sweated under their protective uniforms. Only the sound of bees and the chirping of small birds made any sound.

Inside the cottage Bernard was ready to destroy any signs that he and Hugo had spent nearly a week hidden away. Leaning over, he lit the dry leaves in the centre of his bonfire with his lighter. As he bent over, his car keys dropped out of his shirt pocket down into a pile of wood lying alongside the fire. Bernard scrabbled frantically for them, touching the key ring, only to knock it deeper. Panicking, knowing that he couldn't escape from the area without any means of transport, he failed to notice the speed at which the fire took hold, encouraged by a sudden gust of wind that blew in through the window with the broken panes. In seconds the whole room was ablaze. The wood had been drying out for years. The heat on his back caused Bernard to jump up and turn around. The flames were all around him. He began to scream as he desperately tried to fight his way to the door, only to be beaten back by the fierce heat.

Bernard died very quickly, with one last thought in his mind – what about the child? Would anyone find him?

Helen had gone with Rory to the end of the track. Rory opened a gate to pull off the road and the car they had come in parked a little way along the road. Helen wouldn't remain seated in it as Rory tried to persuade her to do.

The policemen, converging from several different directions, crept closer and closer, watching and waiting for any movement. Inspector Jarvis was ready to order Mr Bernard Smith to come out when there was a sudden flash of flame that appeared to engulf the cottage from floor to roof. In total astonishment the inspector shot out of the undergrowth.

"Take care, sir!" shouted Stockton, as he tried to stop the inspector getting any closer, while following him with his gun raised.

A sound of screaming was heard coming from the cottage. Inspector Jarvis rushed forward.

"The child! There's a child in there!"

The flames were coming from everywhere. In moments, the whole cottage was alight. Glass cracked and popped out of the windows.

The inspector ran towards the open door as though he was going in. Both McDonald and Stockton dropped their weapons and launched themselves upon the inspector.

"No, sir! You can't! You mustn't try – it's too late!"

"Helen's son is in there – I've got to get him out!" he yelled back at them – fighting to get free from their grasp.

"It's too late, inspector. Whoever was in there won't have survived!" –and, as if to confirm that, the screaming stopped.

Inspector Jarvis stopped fighting them. His head dropped in his hands and he began to sob. He'd failed! By being cautious and waiting, he had allowed Helen's son to die a horrible death.

The other policemen came running up. They were helpless to do anything. The fire roared on. One of them called the fire service – but they knew it would only be of little use to solve why the fire had started. By the time they got there, there would be very little left.

Mr Morgan had seen and heard the flames and ran back down the field as fast as his old legs would carry him

Helen and Rory had also seen the fire. Before anyone could stop her, Helen ran off towards the cottage. Too frightened to cry out, she ran past the old barns and on through the trees that concealed the cottage. Rory followed her, too dumbstruck to make a sound. They arrived together.

Rory saw Colin down on his knees and guessed that the fire had killed Bernard and Hugo. He turned and grabbed Helen, holding her tight.

"Hugo? Where's Hugo?" she cried out in despair, trying to dash towards the flames. She looked round at the policemen standing near her.

"He's in there, isn't he?" she whispered. No one answered. No one needed to. The way they were standing told her the worst – and she fainted into Rory's arms.

Chapter 24

"Sit her down, Rory. Push her head down between her knees," the inspector said as he knelt down beside them. "Oh, Helen, I'm so very sorry. It was my fault! If only I hadn't delayed, Hugo might have been alive now," his voice filled with anguish.

Helen couldn't answer. Huge shudders shook her body – then she began to weep.

It was at that moment that one of the policemen from the roadblock came into view, holding the hand of a small boy.

"Mummy, mummy," shouted Hugo. "What happened to the cottage? Did Uncle Bernard burn it down?"

As if in a dream, Helen looked up as she heard the shrill voice of her son.

"Hugo? What are you doing here? I thought you were in there!"

"No, Uncle Bernard made me stay in the car. Where is he?"

"We're not sure son," replied the inspector, meeting Hugo for the first time and seeing that he had his mother's eyes. Realising that Helen was almost hysterical, he said to Hugo, "Come and give your mum a hug, son – she's missed you very much indeed."

Hugo went over to his mother, put his arms round her neck and said, "Hi, mum. Uncle Bernard was going to bring me back to you today. I've really missed you mum – how's Amy?"

Helen buried her head in her small son's shoulder and just sobbed.

"Mum…you said we could go to Eastbourne. Please can we go. I never did get to go in the sea."

"Yes, darling, if you want to – or, what about Disneyland in California? We can go to the beach over there."

"Yes! Great! Mum can I see Michael again – he says he's my cousin."

Helen looked bewildered. "Who's Michael?"

"He's the boy I stayed with before Uncle Bernard took me away in the car."

The inspector walked away to talk to P.C. Dai Thomas.

"Fetch a car as close as possible, and then arrange for someone to take Mrs Brierly and her son to the local hospital. I want her son checked out, and Mrs Brierly is suffering from shock. See that they get there as soon as possible."

"Yes, sir. Shall I phone ahead to get a doctor to stand by?"

"Yes, good idea."

P.C. Thomas contacted one of the policemen still waiting near the main road and asked him to bring a car as far up the track as possible to collect Helen and Hugo.

The inspector turned to Rory and said, "Rory, I think it would be better to get Helen and her son away from here as quickly as we can. I'd like to get them both to hospital for medical treatment. She needs to be treated for shock, and I'd like to know the boy hasn't been abused in any way."

"Yes, you're right. If you tell me where the nearest hospital is, I'll get them there."

"I've arranged for a police car to transport them, but you might want to go with them. I'm also worried about the boy's reaction if he realises Mr Smith is in there," he said, pointing at the cottage.

"Hey, mum! I can hear a fire-engine coming!" shouted Hugo, with excitement. "Can I stay and watch it?"

"No, Hugo," Rory replied gently. "Your mum is not feeling very well. We need to get her to see a doctor."

Hugo's face fell, but he did agree that his mother didn't look well, and so reluctantly, he followed Rory and the policeman who were leading her away from the scene.

Inspector Jarvis was also worried about the farmer, who appeared to be having trouble breathing. As soon as the firemen burst through the trees, he directed one of them to administer oxygen to the old man.

They'd had a tough time getting to the scene of the fire because of the overgrown nature of the track. Unrolling water hoses as they came, the fire crew quickly realised there was little they could do to save the building, but they pumped water on to the cottage and especially on to the surrounding undergrowth to contain the fire and stop it spreading further.

Inspector Jarvis went over to talk to Captain Davies, head of the team of fire fighters, to explain that a man had lost his life inside the cottage. No, they didn't know how the fire had started, but he guessed that the deceased had been responsible.

"Mr Morgan, the farmer who owns the cottage, tells me that it was full of wood collected by an old tramp, who had lived here for about ten years. After this hot summer, it would be as dry as a bone."

Captain Davies shook his head. "It'll be a while before it's cool enough to recover the body – or at least what's left of it."

"Can I leave it to you? I've got a car to check on – hidden in one of those old barns you came past."

"Yes, inspector. Where can I get in touch with you when we get through here?"

Inspector Jarvis gave him several numbers, including his mobile.

Calling his armed force together, he de-briefed them and sent them back to the farmyard where their police van was waiting. Mr Morgan was looking a little better and ready to go home. The six policemen undertook to get him back safely. The inspector watched them go, glad that their skills hadn't been required, because of the danger to Hugo. But he was sad the operation had ended the way it had, with the loss of Mr Smith.

"Damn," he said out loud to himself. "If we'd got here earlier, we could have caught the bastard before he managed to kill himself!"

"Sorry, guv, what did you say?" asked one of the young policemen still in the vicinity.

"Nothing. Just talking to myself. Come on, let's check out the car. Can you call in the Scene of Crime squad to give it the once over?"

"Yes, sir. Do you want them to meet us at the barn?"

"Yes, please."

With a glance over his shoulder, Inspector Jarvis moved away from the cottage that had sheltered Hugo Brierly and Bernard Smith. He walked towards the barns, past the fire engine, where the firemen were still busy. As he hadn't approached the cottage by this route, he was surprised by the number of semi-derelict buildings there were.

On the way he thought about Helen. Since her arrival at the cottage she had neither spoken to him, nor acknowledged his presence. It was as if he hadn't been there. Colin had been so sure of her regard for him that he felt shocked by her indifference. Did she now feel hate for him that he had exposed Hugo to such danger? Had she lost her respect for him? Or – and he hoped it was only this, that she was in such shock herself, she was oblivious to her surroundings.

He had watched Helen stumble away, and his heart went out to her. He wanted, more than anything, to be with her and protect her – but he still had a job to do. First he must begin to investigate Bernard Smith's car and then he had reports to prepare for the various Chief Constables he'd been working with. Reports admitting his failure! He alone had been responsible for the death of Mr Smith. He was only lucky it hadn't been a double tragedy involving an eight-year old boy.

At the barn the SOC officers had arrived and were systematically going about their business. Carefully removing things from the boot of the car, they came across an old mobile phone and found many messages to and from James Brierly detailing his instructions to Bernard in context with the kidnapping.

There it is, thought the inspector, irrefutable proof, if we need it, that Mr Bernard Smith was guilty of the kidnapping. Less than a week ago – but God, it seemed longer.

Inspector Colin Jarvis spoke to the officers briefly. They said they would complete their task and then prepare a report for him. The inspector called out to his driver, who had come up the farm track that he was ready to go back to H.Q.

"Did Mrs Brierly and her son get away safely, do you know?"

"Yes, sir. Webster took them off to Llandrindod Wells. I understand Constable Thomas has arranged for a doctor to be waiting for them."

"Fine. I'll call the hospital from H.Q. and see what they advise. If Mrs Brierly is well enough to travel, I'm sure she'd like to go home. A helicopter is standing by to take her."

"Yes, sir. I'm sorry about the fire. It must have been terrible to see it go up in that way – especially thinking that the little boy was inside."

"Yes, it was terrible. Thanks for your sympathy. Shall we get going? I've some reports to file and a number of phone calls to make."

The police driver drove Inspector Jarvis back to his temporary office and then he, himself, went to make the inspector a pot of tea, for which he thanked him and began making a list of those people he needed to contact. The Chief Constable of Powys was first on his list, and then his own Chief: the hospital to enquire about Helen and Hugo; Sir Ed Stone, her helicopter pilot friend, to ask him to hold on.

Ed was over the moon with delight when the inspector got through to him. "Wonderful! You've rescued Hugo – that's absolutely great. Well Done. How is Helen feeling now?"

Colin Jarvis told him briefly about the fire and the shock of thinking Hugo was in it. "She's at the local hospital at the moment. I tried to have a word with the doctor before calling you, but he was with her and Hugo and said he'd call me back shortly."

"Give me the number at the hospital and I'll call there direct. I'm sure you're very busy, inspector. It'll save you time if I make contact and find out what's happening. And don't be too hard on yourself about the fire – it was perhaps better this way, rather than having to use guns."

"I know – thanks. This is the number of the direct line to the doctor's secretary," he said as he passed it on.

His next two calls to the Chief Constables were much more difficult. He put all the blame on himself. His own Chief was much inclined to be relieved that the child was safe, but asked for a full report as soon as possible.

Colin hadn't forgotten the journalist friend who had kept his promise not to let anything out in the Press and he phoned him to tell him he would brief him later on.

Then there was the call to P.C. Andy Boon, who was still staying with Keith. He would have to break the news to him about his half-brother's untimely death. And, of course, there was James Brierly, the other half-brother. A man he hated. And one who had caused so much pain in the last week. He'd have him behind bars for a very long time – he promised himself.

James! Oh my God! What time was it? Ten minutes to four. The deadline for the transfer of the money to Switzerland – when was it? I must get hold of Rory, he said to himself. I've got to tell him to get Helen to stop the transfer.

As he was reaching for his phone, it rang. "Dr Blacker here, returning your call inspector."

"Thanks Doctor. How is Mrs Brierly? Is she able to talk to me?"

"Yes. She's still a bit upset – but who wouldn't be after the ordeal she's been through? Do you want to talk to her?"

"Yes. No. Perhaps you could just ask her a question for me. Please ask her if she's cancelled the money transfer yet."

There was a short silence, and then the doctor came back on the line. "She says 'no', but her brother-in-law is here with her and he says he will deal with it immediately. In the confusion, he says, everybody had forgotten about it, and he says, he isn't sure whether Mr Bernard Smith deliberately gave them the wrong bank account number or whether it was an accident – but the money was to be send to a British bank – not a Swiss one! While he's doing that, Mrs Brierly says she'd like to speak to you – do you have the time?"

"Yes, of course." There was another pause while the phone was handed over.

Helen came on, sounding a bit groggy. "They've given me something to stop the shakes. I don't know what, but it's made me a bit sleepy. Colin – I'm so sorry I went to pieces out there. I was so terrified I'd lost Hugo – I just didn't know what was happening."

Colin's heart felt it was spinning out of control. "Helen, you've had a terrible shock, it's not surprising you were upset. Do you feel like going home? I've asked Ed to wait to hear from you or me about flying home tonight. Do you want me to tell him to come and get you – or we can send a police car for you. What would you like to do?"

"I'd like to go home. Hugo wants to as well. He's heard his cousins are staying at Ali and Rory's house and he's dying to get back to play with them. Rory's here and he's told me police car is waiting to take us back to the helicopter. He has decided to stay on here and come back with you when you are ready, if that's OK with you?"

"How's Hugo?"

"He's fine. He just said he got a bit bored but he wasn't harmed in any way – thank goodness. He's so excited to be going home by helicopter and says he's going to sit up front! He is asking if we can fly over where the cottage was so he can see the fire. I've told him no. I don't think it has sunk in yet that the man he called Uncle Bernard has died in there."

"Rory's dealing with the money transfer, isn't he?"

"Yes, he's talking to the accountant right now. Apparently, from what I can gather, he was having kittens, not having heard from us. And, Colin – although Bernard was an awful old man, stealing Hugo away from us – I wouldn't have wished that sort of death on him."

"I know you wouldn't – but it would have been a very quick death from smoke inhalation and asphyxiation – he wouldn't have suffered long, and you know, perhaps it was preferable to a long stay in prison at his age, which is what he would have got, you know."

"Yes, perhaps you're right – but it seems terrible anyway. I can't help thinking that Hugo might have been in there too."

"Helen, you mustn't think of that. Hugo is *safe*, and will probably bounce back long before you do – just hold on to that."

"Can I have a word with the Doctor for a moment?"

"Of course. Colin…." she said hesitantly, "you will come and see us soon, won't you?"

"Nothing could keep me away!" he replied, emotionally".

Helen handed the phone to the doctor.

"Is she all right to travel?"

"Yes, I think so. I've given her a mild sedative. I think she's better off in her own bed – away from the memory of all this."

"Thank you."

"And don't worry about going over the area where it all happened. For one thing, I don't think the pilot would be daft enough, and for another,

Mrs Brierly will almost certainly be asleep soon after they are airborne. Oh, just a minute, Mr Johnson would like a word with you inspector."

"Hallo Rory."

"Hi Colin. Thank goodness you remembered about the money. I'd switched off Helen's mobile and her poor accountant was going mad, not knowing what to do. The relief when I phoned him and told him about Hugo – the poor man was almost in tears. Anyway, he pulled himself together and said he'd phone the bank immediately."

"I was just thinking about telling Keith and James about their brother's death when I remembered the deadline." Then he added, "You'll see her into the helicopter, won't you? I can't come myself – I've too many loose ends to tie up."

Rory replied that he would and Inspector Jarvis said, "Please tell her I'll phone her at home tomorrow when she's had a good night's sleep."

"I'll do that. How are you getting back? I can stay on if you like, and perhaps we can travel back together. Also, would you like me to talk to Keith and tell him about his brother's death?"

"That would be great if you could. P.C. Andy Booth is with him and will help you to break the news. Look, I don't know how late I'll be. Got a lot of tidying up to do here."

"Don't worry about that, I'll wait for you. Shall I come to your HQ or wait at the hotel?"

"At the hotel would be better".

As a result of one of his calls, orders went out to make sure Mr James Brierly did not get any news of his son's rescue, or the death of his half-brother, Bernard. Inspector Jarvis had decided to try again to get James to own up to his involvement in the kidnap plan. He knew he'd got plenty of evidence that he had been behind the whole plot, but he wanted to make James squirm and feel the sort of pain he'd inflicted on his wretched family.

The fire crew Captain phoned in to say that although the fire at the cottage was now out, it was still too hot to do any investigation into what had started the blaze, or to recover the body. "It'll be tomorrow before we can get into the ruins."

"Right, I'll arrange for police cover to guard the cottage overnight. Thanks Captain Davies – I appreciate your help."

"It's OK Inspector. By the way, how are the mother and her son? I understand you had them taken to hospital for a check-up."

"They're fine. Hugo, the little boy, seems to be in great spirits. His mother is still pretty shaken up, but they're on their way home right now."

"Good. I'll pass the message on to the rest of the crew."

"Are there any of my men still there?"

"Yes, a couple of men from the local station, P.C. Dai Thomas and P.C. Paul Chason are still on site."

"Thanks. Can I have a word with one of them?"

Dai Thomas came on a moment later.

"Police Constable Thomas here, sir."

"Thomas, I'd like you and Chason to remain there for the moment so that the fire crew can stand down. I'll get relief cover for you as soon as I can."

"I'd like to volunteer to stay here sir. I feel a bit responsible for not being available last night."

"OK constable. I'll get food etc sent out to you. Can you please tell Captain Davies that I am planning to go back down south to Wiltshire this evening and so could he please email his report through to me. Thanks for your help. Good bye."

Inspector Jarvis hung up the phone, very glad that Rory had offered to stay for a bit longer in order to accompany him back as far as the manor where a police car could pick him up and take him on to Dover where James Brierly was being held.

A very capable sergeant was busy taking statements from Mr Morgan and his wife so that P.C. Thomas could sit and write his report while guarding the remains of the burnt out cottage.

Rory arrived at the police station ready to set off for Wiltshire. Inspector Jarvis was just finishing a phone call to the local Police Chief, thanking him for his support and pointing out that, although the national newspapers hadn't got wind of the story yet, there would be an onslaught when they did find out. At this time, more officers would be needed to keep them away from the location of the former cottage.

Desk cleared, the inspector left a list of numbers on which he could be contacted and went out to the police car where Rory was waiting. He'd decided he would get on with his own report in the car heading south.

Chapter 25

olin and Rory climbed tiredly into the back of the unmarked police car. As the driver started the engine the inspector leaned forward and asked him if he knew of a pub where they could get something to eat quickly. Both men were exhausted but felt they should eat before the long journey back south.

"A mile down the road Sir, it's a grand little pub and their steak pies are really good".

"Sounds great to us. Take us there please", replied the inspector. "A pie and a pint, that OK for you Rory?

Upon arrival they were led into an almost deserted dining room area. Colin invited the driver to join them, but he said he'd already eaten and would go into the snug where a friend of his was sitting.

"Right you are. We'll be as quick as we can".

Alison had called Rory to tell him that Hugo and Helen had arrived home safely. Helen still very drawn, but was relaxed. "I've got her sitting outside on a garden chair, sipping a gin and tonic. She's just enjoying watching Hugo chase around with his cousins. He certainly doesn't appear to be any worse for his ordeal," she told Rory.

"I'm on my way to you where I'll be dropped off by Colin, he will be heading on down to Dover. I don't know what time we'll get to you, but don't worry, we're eating on the way. I'll see you later," replied Rory.

During the meal, Rory told Colin about the conversation he'd had with Keith.

"I called the number and your Sergeant Andy answered the phone. I told him about the death of Keith's brother. He immediately asked if Hugo was OK. I said yes and did he think Keith was up to talking to me. After a moment or two, Keith came on the phone. I told him the whole story. He was so quiet I wondered whether he was listening when I heard a muffled cry. The poor old man was taking it all in. He said he was sad about his brother but very happy to hear Hugo was safe. He was a nice little boy, he said and his grandson Michael had got on really well with him. In the end I could hear the emotion in his voice. I don't know whether he was crying about the death of his brother, or relief that everything had turned out right. He asked about Helen and I told him she and Hugo would be home again in Wiltshire by now. He just said thank you and hung up".

"Yes, he is a poor old man. I liked him when I interviewed him, but to lose one brother and have the other in police custody is going to be hard for him to cope with in one day".

After the meal and heading along the M4 and the M25, Inspector Jarvis dozed off. Rory let him sleep, reckoning he'd have a hard night ahead of him talking to James. They had already discussed what the inspector planned to do. He was going to try and shock James into admitting his guilt by letting him believe that both his brother *and* his son were dead.

"I really hope it hurts the bastard!" Rory had said vehemently. "He deserves it."

They reached the manor house soon after midnight. Another police car was there ready to take the inspector to Dover, where James was being held waiting for Inspector Jarvis to arrive.

At 2:00 am James was brought into an interview room to face the inspector across a bare table. James's solicitor had been dragged in. He'd objected of course, but was told that the police had something they needed to inform his client about and it couldn't wait until the morning.

"Sit down Mr Brierly I have something to tell you."

"Well I've got nothing to tell *you!*" said James belligerently.

Ignoring him, Inspector Jarvis went on, "We've found your brother and your son."

"About time too."

"You're not listening are you Mr Brierly? We've found them, but there's been a terrible accident."

James sat up. "What sort of accident?"

"The cottage they've been living in has burnt down – unfortunately there was no way of escaping from the fire."

"*You* set it on fire deliberately, didn't you? *You* couldn't pin the kidnap on me, so you've killed my half- brother *and* my son – just to get even – haven't you – *you filthy bastard!*"

The solicitor interrupted. "Mr Brierly, you don't have to say anything."

Inspector Jarvis ignored the solicitor and went on, "Your brother, who ran off with your son. That wasn't part of the plan – was it Mr Brierly? You planned for him to do all the dirty work and then you were planning to run off with all the money – *weren't you?* Your *son* would be with his mother and sister right now, *wouldn't he* – if you hadn't decided to kidnap *your own son!*"

James sat staring into space. Inspector Jarvis continued. "I heard the screams myself. Screams coming from inside the cottage – *from inside the flames!* The screaming didn't go on for long – death came quickly."

James began looking wildly around him, "He wasn't supposed to take him away! He was supposed to bring him to France. It was his fault! I never told him to run off. That *stupid old man* decided to change *my* plans...."

"Mr Brierly," cautioned the solicitor. "Don't incriminate yourself!"

James continued as though he hadn't heard, "It was his fault that he died! *His fault – do you hear?*" shouted James. "I don't care about him – I was going to dump him anyway – but why did he have to take Hugo with him?"

The solicitor tried to intervene again, but James was almost hysterical with rage about his brothers, and he poured out his anger trying to put the blame on them, but in the process of doing so, he gave away his involvement in the whole scheme.

At this moment Inspector Jarvis truly believed James was insane – and from the look of him, so did the solicitor, who had given up trying to curb James's confession, which was being taken down verbatim by a police stenographer.

He'll plead guilty on the grounds of insanity, thought the inspector. He's been so twisted up by his mother, that I think he really believes he has a right to Helen's money,

The duty solicitor leant forward and asked, "So both his brother and son are dead?"

"Did I actually say that? No, I don't think so. Oh yes, his brother is dead. We're still waiting for the remains of the fire to cool down enough to bring his body out. We'll have to do DNA tests on what's left to make sure it is Mr Bernard Smith. But his son? No, I imagine he'll be fast asleep in his bed at home at the moment."

"Inspector Jarvis! That was not on. You led the poor man to believe his son had died as well!"

"Did I? Well just you understand this, Mr Evans," answered the inspector in an angry voice, "it was only by the Grace of God, that the child *wasn't* in there! And let me tell you we have made some interesting discoveries about Mr Brierly from his past that will put him away for a very long time, if the bad guys don't catch up with him first. Right take him away and lock him up! Good night Mr Evans. You can come and visit your client tomorrow and discuss whether he pleads guilty by means of insanity."

With that Inspector Jarvis got wearily to his feet – almost rocking with tiredness.

"Get one of the drivers to run me back to Wiltshire, will you? I'm too tired to drive myself".

With a quick 'good night' to the duty staff, he left for the journey back to his own home.

Chapter 26

he two families had stayed on at the manor house for another 10 days, it was easier to keep the press at a distance. The main front gate was locked and another entrance at the rear of the grounds had been padlocked, while a police car patrolled the grounds. As the inspector had foretold, the press were eager to get interviews and in the end they decided that if they had a formal press conference where they could tell people what had happened, barring anything that needed to be kept under wraps pending the trial, it would at least placate the thirst for information. So, Helen, Alison and Rory and her barrister, sat behind a desk with the press facing them, the three of them very nervous.

The questions came thick and fast as to how Helen had felt when she knew her son had been kidnapped? When did she think her ex-husband had been involved? How did they work out where Hugo had been taken and how did she feel when she saw the cottage burning down and thought her son was inside?

Helen shuddered at this question and Rory answered for her, "My sister-in-law is still very traumatised, so please forgive her if she doesn't answer this question. I will speak for her as I was with her at the time. We were a bit away from the cottage and couldn't see what was happening and then heard a shout about the fire and my sister-in- law just shot off along the track. At that time, we had no idea what had happened or if anyone was inside. As we reached the cottage, we could see it was burning from end to end and realised someone, or some people were in the inferno. Naturally my sister-in-law went into shock. In what seemed like an hour, but was probably only a minute or two, a policeman appeared holding Hugo's hand. He'd found him asleep on the back seat of the car".

"Mrs Brierly, how do you feel about the death of the kidnapper?"

Helen almost whispered, "I know what he did was evil, but my son says he was very kind to him and looked after him well. So, all I can say is that I am sorry he died, but perhaps it was better than him spending years in gaol".

Rory chipped in next, "We are not able to say, pending the case, very much, so all we can say is that we feel he was encouraged by his brother. Thank you for coming, and please can you give us some space to get over the extraordinary pressure we have experienced during the kidnapping".

After the ten days were up, both families headed to their own homes as their children needed to return to school.

Helen and Colin had spoken on the phone but did not meet up again until early July when the two families, including Colin went to the manor house for a long weekend.

There had been so much going on after the arrest of James. Solicitors and barristers, the police and reports about James's mental health had taken up a lot of their time. After days and weeks of questioning by psychiatrists and analysts, it was deemed that James was not fit to go before a judge and jury. That he was guilty no-one doubted because he had told everyone that he had planned it, but it was his brother's fault it had gone wrong and it was his fault he'd died in the fire. Bernard was supposed to drive Hugo to France – but he'd gone off on his own, disobeying James.

After numerous discussions with experts and legal advice, James was sent to a secure mental institution until, if ever, he was able to stand trial.

Helen and her family had quietly become acquainted with her half-brother Keith and his family. Tears had been shed and as Hugo had said, she did like Michael, Keith's grandson.

Colin had arrived later than the family and was greeted by everybody with pleasure.

All the children were playing happily, supervised by Alison, in the indoor swimming pool their grandfather had built many years before, so Colin suggested he and Helen went for a walk – he had something he wanted to tell her. He took her hand and Helen said she had some exciting news too. They headed towards the summerhouse overlooking the lake. Colin pulled out two chairs for them to sit on. He took her hand again.

"You go first Helen, tell me what's happened".

"Rory and I have been talking about the cottage in France. It is still in my name, although I was going to make it over to James in the divorce settlement. The house part of the cottage is really quite small, however, a completely empty barn attached to the end furthest away from the road is huge. Rory has been doing some drawings. He says he will need somewhere to stay when he goes on the wine buying trips and has suggested the barn could be turned into a large extension with three more bedrooms and bathrooms, a very large kitchen/dining room and a conservatory on the end. There is room for a reasonable sized swimming pool, not huge but large enough for the kids. It can get very hot in that part of France in the summer, and a hot tub for the winter, when it gets very cold -15c last year! We have room for a barbecue, and we already have outdoor furniture".

Helen continued in her excitement, "Rory has found a small par three golf course only a few miles away from the cottage. He says he will take Hugo and his son George there. It will take a while to do the work on the barn, but Rory has offered to take the boys to have lessons at his golf club over here. He told me you are a golfer as well".

"I play very rarely now but I am hoping to play a lot more in future – especially at the course Rory mentioned at Chaorce"

What do you think of the idea of extending the cottage?"

"It sounds amazing. Shall I tell you, my news?"

"Yes please".

"I have also been talking to Rory - lots in fact. I have become very disillusioned with being in the police, especially the branch I am in. The kidnap of Hugo was the end for me. After twenty-five years I am ready to retire. Anyway, Rory's wine import business is growing fast, and he has asked me to join him as a partner. He wants to expand into South American wines and needs someone over here to handle all day to day work with importing the various wines. I have said yes. I think I'll have to go on some wine tasting courses because I have very little knowledge about the production of wine. I know what I like, but not why".

"Oh Colin, I am so glad – but why didn't Rory tell me himself?"

"He wanted me to break the news that I will be leaving the police force and joining him. We have already found a suitable warehouse. It makes sense that we keep it in the family, after all he will be my brother-in-law as well".

Helen just held his hand a little tighter while she turned at him and gave him a delighted smile. Colin was already looking at her and watching her reaction They both knew it was going to be fine, and smiled their happiness.

Her father would get his dearest wish after all.